MAGGIE AN...

by

SARAH FISHER

Maggie and the Master published in 2003 & 2011 by
Chimera Books Ltd
PO Box 152
Waterlooville
Hants
PO8 9FS
United Kingdom

Printed and bound in the UK by
Cox & Wyman, Reading.

ISBN 978-1-903931-52-3

This novel is fiction – in real life practice safe sex

This book is sold subject to the condition that it shall not, by way of trade or otherwise, be lent, resold, hired out or otherwise circulated without the publisher's prior written consent in any form of binding or cover other than that in which it is published, and without a similar condition being imposed on the subsequent purchaser.

The characters and situations in this book are entirely imaginary and bear no relation to any real person or actual happening.

Copyright © Sarah Fisher

The right of Sarah Fisher to be identified as author of this book has been asserted in accordance with section 77 and 78 of the Copyrights Designs and Patents Act 1988.

MAGGIE AND THE MASTER

Sarah Fisher

Chimera *(kī-mîr'ə, kĭ-)* a creation of the imagination, a wild fantasy

It was a dungeon. There was no other word for it. In one corner was an awful rack, and in another a large, foreboding cross-shaped frame. The walls were hung with whips and crops and gags and manacles, clamps and clips and all manner of other things, many of which Maggie didn't recognise and had no idea what they might be used for.

She turned to Guido. 'Let me go back,' she pleaded, unnerved by the ominous room. 'I'll eat my dinner, I will, it was a mistake. Just take me back. Honestly Guido, it was a silly mistake.'

Guido's smile widened. 'You're right about that,' he said, 'but it's too late to go back now. I suggest you cooperate, because if you don't it will be worse for you… a lot worse.'

Chapter One

Max Jordan smiled at Katya and ran a hand over her cheek and then down to her shoulders, his fingers moving slowly, tracing the curve of her breasts and the faultless contours of her pink nipples. Under his touch first one and then the other hardened into tight buds.

Eyes downcast, feet apart, hands behind her back; over the past few months Katya had become the very epitome of the dutiful slave, and thought Max, was all the better for it. Since he had completed her training she was altogether calmer, more self-assured, even more beautiful than when they first met. She was the picture of elegance when they were out together and completely wanton, his to command and enjoy, when they were in private.

Katya had been a pleasure to train – a natural submissive, despite her initial resistance. The girl had been remarkably quick to understand what was required of her, and helping her to find the way past her natural resistance, finding the way to make her – and others like her – compliant and eager to serve him was what Max Jordan did best.

She trembled slightly as he stroked his fingertips over her belly and parted the lips of her sex to enter and explore. There was no hint of resistance; rather he sensed her eagerness for his caress, his attentions, his dominance.

Since they'd met Max had helped Katya unlock the natural submissiveness she had hidden away for so long. Now her body and her mind and her very soul were his to use and abuse and pleasure exactly as and when he chose, to give to whom he wanted, to deny her, to indulge her, to beat her until her screams filled the room and lingered in his dreams.

Tonight he thought how exquisite she looked, totally naked, her mons shaved and oiled for his approval, her face betraying just a hint of make-up to emphasise her full lips and deep brown eyes, her short blonde hair brushed off her face making her look almost elfin. Her black and silver collar was cut deep to accentuate the line of her slender neck, and the matching lead – well, he intended to hold on to the lead for just a little longer.

'You understand what is happening, my little one?' he asked tenderly. Max had no need to shout or bark instructions at her; Katya had long since learned the penalties of disobedience and the rewards of complete submission.

'Yes... Master.' Katya's voice was low and soft and faltered over the words.

He smiled again, and tipping her face up to his pressed his lips to hers. He could see the glitter of tears in her eyes and felt the trembling flutter of her lips like a trapped butterfly against his.

'You will be well taken care of, my precious,' he said. 'I wouldn't have it otherwise.'

She didn't have a chance to reply.

'Master, Mr Gilbert is here.'

Max swung round at the sound of his housekeeper's voice. 'Wonderful, Mrs Griffin, would you show him in, please?'

He stepped away from Katya and hung the lead up on the hook alongside her. 'Spread you legs a little wider, my dear; Jack will want to inspect his new toy.' Without lifting her head Katya did exactly as instructed. Six months earlier she would have fought him, answered him back or made some smart remark, and it was interesting how the crop and a firm hand could teach a girl the virtues of silence and complete obedience. For a moment, master or not, Max's heart ached. He would miss her.

'Ah, Max, there you are. How's life treating you?'

Max crossed the room to greet his guest. 'Fine, Jack, how nice to see you again. Come in and make yourself at home. Would you like a drink?'

'Scotch would be good.'

'How was the drive?'

'Very good, hardly any traffic...' Their exchange of pleasantries was brief; Max could see that Jack's attentions were already elsewhere. 'So this is the little creature you told me about, is it?' he said, walking over to the corner where Katya was secured.

Soft lights picked out the delicate glow of her skin; she was so perfect, so very delicately made that she almost looked like a statue standing there.

'Indeed,' said Max. Her delicate appearance belied the way her body writhed beneath his like a hungry animal, the way she opened up under his touch, the silky wetness that pooled in her sex, so much that often as he buried his cock deep inside her it seeped down her thighs.

Jack pursed his lips and looked the girl up and down thoughtfully, as if appraising livestock. 'Not bad... not bad at all,' he said, stepping a little closer. 'May I?'

'Help yourself,' said Max, pouring a generous measure of scotch into the two tumblers on a side table. 'After all, after tonight she'll be all yours. Assuming of course that you want another of my girls in your harem?'

Jack laughed as he surveyed Katya. She stood perfectly still, just as she had been taught, dark eyes resolutely downcast. 'Hardly a harem, Max, and besides, your girls are always so well schooled. I've never had the stamina for breaking and training myself, whereas you – well, it's a gift. A gift we are all pleased to enjoy.'

'Flattery will not reduce the price,' said Max wryly.

'As if I would think such a thing,' said Jack with a grin. He took the drink offered him, and fishing the ice from the glass drew it down over Katya's throat and then traced a slow glittering line to her belly, before easing it slowly across the contours of her sex.

The girl shivered, and with her eyes closed threw back her head as it passed over her clit, letting out a gasp as his fingers found the heat of her.

'Wet already,' he said admiringly. 'My, my, but you train them so very well, dear fellow.'

'Anticipation plays a great part in this game, Jack; you should know that by now,' said Max. 'As a slave Katya already has some idea of what to expect. The secret is to tell them just enough to feed the imagination, but not enough to spoil the surprise.'

'So you keep telling me, in which case let's not disappoint her, eh?' Jack said, pushing the ice home, forcing it deep inside her, his fingers parting her outer lips to find his mark. Katya gasped.

Max closed his eyes for an instant, imagining the way the well-toned muscles of Katya's cunt would close tight around those invading fingers, imagined the sensation as the ice instantly began to melt, glistening rivulets trickling down the insides of Katya's taut thighs, water mixing with the musky perfume of her body.

He could see the girl's cheeks reddening furiously and smiled to himself. It was a fine balance to unleash the wanton in a girl whilst still retaining a certain coy self-consciousness, an ability to feel shame mixed amongst the most extreme pleasures.

Jack's finger explored deeper still, moving

rhythmically while his thumb lifted to brush her clitoris, and in the stillness of the room Katya let out a long moan, a heady mixture of pleasure and humiliation.

Pulling out, Jack took the lead down from the hook and snapped it tight. 'Get on your hands and knees, bitch. I want to see exactly what it is I'm getting for my money.'

Wordlessly Katya complied, her head down, hips raised, knees well apart so that every inch of her body was available to the man Max had so recently sold her to. Jack left her there a moment or two so that the extent of her submission was emphasised.

He then crouched beside her and ran his hands over her breasts, cradling their weight in his palms, teasing and pinching the nipples, before working farther back over her flanks and thighs.

'What's this, not a bruise, nor a single welt?' he mused conversationally, passing a hand over the ample curve of her buttocks before turning back to Max.

'No, I thought you might prefer to mark her yourself.'

Jack laughed. 'How well you know me,' he said. 'What shall we say, then? Twenty with the cane? Or perhaps the crop? Or maybe just an old fashioned spanking to begin with?'

'Whichever you prefer, Jack, you know we can accommodate them all here.' On the floor between them Katya remained totally motionless.

Jack glanced at the wall of Max's study, hung with the instruments of his craft. The man smiled appreciatively. 'That's a rather handsome cat you have there. It's new, isn't it?'

'Handcrafted by a dear friend of mine,' Max confirmed. 'Would you care to try it out?' He passed it across, and Jack hefted the weight and tried a couple of practice sweeps to judge how the weight lay before taking off his jacket and moving behind Katya.

'Twenty?' he said again, and Max nodded. Katya was certainly not afraid of pain, although like most of the slaves he'd trained over the years her relationship with it was ambivalent – love and hate combined in a single instant. Max could see a sheen of sweat on the girl's back and detected the slight tremble in her legs as Jack prepared.

His first strike was clumsy, missing her buttocks and instead winding the snapping tendrils around her thighs, biting the silky skin.

'One,' she sobbed, grimacing.

The cat hissed again.

'Two,' she gasped, Jack hitting her squarely across her bottom, making her rock forward. He waited until she was still, waited for that instant when she just started to relax and then struck again, lower this time so the tails cut across the tops of her thighs.

'Three,' she squealed.

Max felt his pulse quicken as she writhed under the cat's attentions, letting the pain echo through her. He could almost feel the crack of it like some electrical charge that lit a fire in his belly. Damn she looked beautiful; her skin reacted quickly, the bite of the cat's tails already lifting narrow stripes and red kisses on her creamy white flesh. Tonight he and Jack would share her and tomorrow she would be gone forever.

As Jack lay on each stroke Katya counted diligently, between cries and strangled sobs, calling out her punishment. When at last he was done she crawled over to him, her eyes bright with tears, and kissed the cat that lay in his hands, thanking him for its hot caress before returning to the position on all fours.

Jack, breathless, eyes bright with excitement, ran his fingers through her hair and then began to stroke her burning flesh. She mewled like a kitten and pressed against him as he worked over the welts, caught up in the heat and power of the pain. Using the juices from her sex he wetted the tight puckering of her bottom and without prelude began to explore her most secret places – places that until now had been Max's alone.

Katya whimpered as he pushed a finger into her bottom, and Max knew her pleasure was mixed with a potent sense of violation, although she knew better than to protest.

Then Jack unfastened his fly and with one seamless motion drove his throbbing cock deep into the girl's tight sex, his finger still buried deep in her rear. Instinctively her back dipped to meet him as he drove deeper still.

Max smiled; it fell to her new master to have the first choice of pleasures and explore his new prize, after all, he had paid well for the privilege. But Max had known her first, brought her to this place, this state of sweet surrender, and nothing and nobody would ever take that away from him.

Contentedly he settled on a chair in front of Katya, and with no fuss guided his aching cock deep into her waiting mouth. Her impatient tongue ran around the tip, teasing his shaft, working feverishly back and forth between it and the single eye before drawing him deep. He eased back, letting her pleasure him. He was going to miss Katya.

As if reading his mind, between gritted teeth, Jack said, 'What are you going to do once she's gone, Max?'

The man smiled. 'Don't you worry about me, Jack; they say when the student is ready the master will appear, and trust me, in my experience it works the other way around as well. A new girl will turn up soon enough. Katya is just the latest. There is always another...' Looking at the face of his companion Max knew he might as well be talking to himself. Buried to the balls in the girl's compliant body, Jack snorted and threw back his head, pleasure suffusing his heavy features and driving away any further need for conversation.

'So, what do you think of this?' said Kay, executing a faultless pirouette across the sitting room.

Maggie Howard looked up from her book at her new lodger and grinned. 'You're not seriously going to go out in that, are you?'

Kay's shapely body looked as if it had been poured into the tiny rubber dress she was wearing, with its thin straps and low-cut neckline. The dress ended six inches above her knees, showing off a good tan and shapely, slim legs, enhanced by high black patent stilettos. With her long blonde hair twisted up into a French pleat, tendrils hanging down to frame her features, Kay looked as if she had just stepped out of some erotic fantasy.

'Certainly am,' she said, handing Maggie a cloth and a spray bottle. 'Mike bought it for me as a present; we're going to some new club over in Moorville. Don't wait up.'

'I wasn't planning to. What's this?' said Maggie, peering down at the bottle. Mike had to be at least ten years older than Kay and sexy in a dark, predatory way that Maggie found both incredibly intimidating and hugely exciting, not that she intended to share that fact with Kay, who was totally besotted with him.

'Latex polish. I want you to buff me up.'

Maggie lifted an eyebrow. 'Meaning what, exactly?'

Kay laughed. 'Polish me; you need loads of talcum powder to get these things on and it kills the shine. Go on, I can't reach.'

Maggie obliged. Although it felt odd to polish something that gave and wriggled and giggled under her touch, but even so a couple of sprays and a whisk over from the cloth and the little rubber dress glowed with a deeply satisfying patina, emphasising the ripe curves and plains of Kay's gym-honed body.

'This would make a great subject for your column,' said Kay, checking her appearance in the mirror.

'What would?'

'Sex under wraps, fetish stuff; you know, whips and chains and leather. Bondage and rubber.' Kay's eyes widened mischievously. 'This new club would be just the place for a bit of research.'

Maggie shook her head. 'I write a lifestyle section, Kay; mid-30's angst, looking for Mr Right, getting a cheap loan to buy the car of your dreams, building a garden, buying a sofa. And anyway, all that kind of stuff, whips and things, it's a joke, isn't it?'

Kay smiled. 'If you say so,' she said. 'Tell you what, I'll give you a couple of website addresses, go and take a look and then tell me what you think. It's another world out there. People who treat sex as a hobby – an addictive game, worth playing well.'

Maggie pulled her best sceptical face, at which point the doorbell rang. 'Prince Charming?' she suggested.

'I should think so, unless you're expecting someone.'

'Hah – don't rub it in unless you want me to double your rent.'

Giggling, Kay picked up the black leather coat Mike had bought her the week before and went to answer the door, while Maggie turned her attention back to the book. She could hear muffled voices in the hall and waited for the sound of the door to close and for silence to descend again.

She'd been divorced for almost two years, and

although generally life was better – there being nowhere lonelier or more soul destroying than a bad relationship – any lingering optimism about how good life would be out on the far side had long since faded.

Own house, own job, own lodger taken in to make ends meet. Maggie sighed; it wasn't such an exciting story as she'd imagined. It wasn't that she was short of men, it was just that she was short of the *right* men.

Maggie glanced unseeing at her novel, wondering what was taking Kay and Prince Charming so long, hoping they hadn't decided on a quickie in the hall before going clubbing.

Kay put her head back around the door.

'What, don't tell me the pumpkin and six has broken down already,' said Maggie.

'No, Mike said that if you're at a loose end tonight maybe you'd like to come along with us.'

Maggie laughed. 'Are you serious? What, in my pyjamas?'

'Don't be so daft. I'll lend you something. I've got loads of things upstairs.'

'Thanks,' Maggie said, 'but I really don't feel like it tonight. You go and have a good time.'

'He meant it,' Kay said. 'It would do you good to get out. Treat it as research.'

'I'm touched, but I'd feel totally out of place,' said Maggie flatly. 'And besides, I hate playing gooseberry.'

Kay wrinkled her nose. 'Okay, but here…' she pulled a card out of her handbag and scribbled something on it. 'Go and have a look. Whatever you want, whatever your wildest dreams, you can find it on this site – really. It's where I found Mike.'

Maggie smiled indulgently and took the card. 'And that's meant to be a recommendation?'

Kay smiled, waved, and was gone.

Maggie glanced down at the card, intending to drop it in the bin. 'Darksecrets-dot-com,' she read aloud, and then smiled. What the hell had she got to lose? After all, Simon in the office had asked her out for coffee just last week; Simon Faraday with his thinning hair and bad teeth; Simon who seemed to think he was doing her a colossal favour by paying her any attention at all.

She glanced up at the clock; there was still time enough to do a couple of hours work before turning in, although it seemed like a pretty poor way to spend a Friday evening.

She looked at the phone, wondering who to call. Simon had told her she could ring him any time. She got to her feet and headed up to her office; she could always pick up her email too and maybe just take a quick look at Darksecrets. After all, there was no harm in looking, was there?

Max Jordan rolled back amongst the tangle of sheets, sated. As she had been taught, Katya rested her head on his hairy belly, and took his spent cock in her mouth to lick away the traces of both his excitement and her own.

During the long hot evening Max and Jack had shared her in every possible way, using her arse, her mouth, her hands, her face, her breasts, and her cunt, taking themselves and Katya to the very edge of oblivion. Finally Jack had cried enough, his body slick with sweat, his eyes rimmed with fatigue.

Tonight Katya would sleep between them, ready and eager to please if either man woke and had need of her.

Max groaned softly as her tongue worked its own particular magic over his shaft and balls. Some masters preferred their slaves to sleep on the floor, or be bound or chained to a low bed or mattress beside them, or even kept in separate quarters, but Max always enjoyed sleeping with his possessions. He relished feeling the soft flesh of an enslaved girl curled up against him. It strengthened the bond between master and slave, certainly in the early stages, and taught them what pleasures he expected from a submissive.

There was nothing better than to be roused from sleep in the early hours by the caress of eager lips around his semi-hard cock, or to be able to sink barely conscious into the compliant body of a slave taught that his pleasure was paramount.

In his heyday Max liked the girls to come to his room in rotation or in twos or threes, and he would use them as he saw fit. Now he had to take them one at a time, although it still seemed that he had more stamina than the younger Jack.

He stroked Katya's hair back off her face and pulled her up to him. 'Sleep, little one,' he whispered, and without another word she settled down with her head on his chest. He reached over and before extinguishing the light took a long look at his slave. The last thing he saw before the darkness embraced them was the contented smile on Katya's lips.

Kay was right; it was like another world. Maggie stared at the computer screen completely absorbed in the images on the screen, cradling a mug of coffee. It was nearly three in the morning and she had been surfing Darksecrets and links to various other sites for the best part of four hours. What she found there had taken her breath away. All her life, in her darkest fantasies, Maggie had imagined what it might be like to be used and desired and taken by a dominant man, not that she would ever tell Kay that – she had barely dared acknowledge it to herself. And they were here, all her fantasies and more besides, laid bare.

She took a sip of coffee, wishing it were something

stronger. Wasn't that why she married Barry, thinking, hoping he was a dominant male? Hadn't she been looking for a man who would instinctively understand what she needed, a man to look after her, a man to control her, a man who would see her as his possession and relish her submission?

Maggie reddened furiously as the thoughts formed. There was a part of her, a part she had long denied, that wanted a man to use her body, to make her do all those things she had always wanted to do but was too afraid to. Perhaps it wasn't too late to find what she had always known had to be out there, somewhere.

Maggie stared at the page that would let her post a profile in the contact section of the site. What had she got to lose? She didn't have to answer the replies if she got any; she would be anonymous. They wouldn't give out her email address or any personal details. Maggie bit her lip and then began to type, slowly considering every word carefully.

Not long out of a long-term relationship, I'm looking to explore some of the fantasies that have haunted me all my life. I want a real man. A man who understands me. A man who... She paused, wondering how best to put it. *A man who can help me find what I truly am.* She typed with a surety she didn't feel.

Before her courage failed her she added details of her size and age, then watched as the words appeared on the screen, and then very quickly closed the computer down before she had a chance to change her mind. If anyone ever found out about the ad she'd bluff it out, tell them it was research for an article or a story – anything but the truth.

The following morning when Maggie got downstairs, Mike was sitting at the kitchen table drinking coffee.

'Hi, late night?' he said, looking her up and down.

She smiled uncomfortably under his scrutiny. She knew she looked unkempt. 'I didn't realise you were staying,' she said, as lightly as she could manage.

'You don't mind, do you?'

Maggie shook her head. 'No, as long as you don't make a habit of it.'

Kay came in, carrying the post. 'Morning,' she beamed. 'Did you take a look at Darksecrets, then?'

Maggie had already worked out what to say. 'Yes, actually I did, and you're right, it really is amazing. It would make a great article.'

Kay grinned and settled on Mike's lap. It was impossible to ignore the way her nipples pressed through the thin fabric of her T-shirt. 'See, I told you so.'

'Okay, so I was wrong,' Maggie acknowledged.

Across the table Mike looked at her, his expression very different from the puppyish look on Kay's face. Maggie tried very hard not to notice the possessive way his hand rested on Kay's thigh, although as he met Maggie's eye she couldn't help wondering what it was he saw in her face. Did he see her envy, or perhaps her fear?

'Actually, I know someone you should meet,' he said.

Maggie returned his gaze as steadily as she could. 'Really and who would that be?'

'A friend of mine, he taught me everything I know, he's a very interesting man. I'm sure you'll find he's exactly what you're looking for, and maybe visa versa.'

The way Mike spoke hit a raw nerve and Maggie felt her stomach churn. 'To be honest, I'm not sure exactly what I'm looking for, Mike, but if you leave me his number I might give him a ring some time,' she said.

Mike smiled and added milk to his coffee. 'Oh, that

isn't how it works,' he said. 'No, I'll tell him about you, and if he's interested then he'll make contact. Did you put an ad up on the Darksecrets site?'

This time Maggie did blush. 'Yes, I thought it might help with my research.'

'In that case give me the nickname you used.'

'Curious,' said Maggie.

Mike grinned. 'As good a name as any, although you know what curiosity did, don't you?'

Maggie picked up her drink; she couldn't bring herself to reply.

'Hello Maggie.'

It was a week later, Friday evening, and Maggie was curled up on the sofa in front of the television. Kay hadn't come home and left a message on the answer machine to say she wasn't likely to be back until Sunday evening, so Maggie had plans to indulge herself. During the week she made up her mind that Mike's offer had been at worst a bad joke and at best an attempt to humour her.

'Hello, who is this?' she asked, muting the television.

'Mike gave me your number.' The man spoke with a soft Irish lilt, his tone low and even, which was both compelling and oddly disturbing.

Maggie felt her pulse quicken. 'Mike? Kay's Mike?'

'An interesting way to describe him; Mike is one of my more able students. He told me you're curious, Maggie.'

She was unsure of what he expected her to say, if anything.

'The thing is, Maggie, do you know what you're curious about?'

She took a deep breath, wondering if she dare tell him; the silence yawned as deep as the ocean and

Maggie sensed he had no intention of filling the void.

'There are things... things I've always imagined doing... being part of,' she eventually confessed, wondering what on earth possessed her to tell a total stranger the secrets she had kept hidden for so long. 'Things I've always wondered about, fantasised about. And I write... I was hoping to maybe do an article, about those things, maybe.'

'Things,' he repeated in the same low tone. 'What sort of things, Maggie?'

'I can't tell you,' she blustered. 'I can't...' the words dried in her throat as she realised she longed to tell him but couldn't. 'I don't know how to.'

'Don't worry,' he said. 'I'm sure we can find a way to help you discuss your thoughts and dreams.' He paused. 'We should meet. Sunday, we'll meet for lunch.'

'The thing is...' Maggie began, trying to come up with a plausible excuse.

'Good, I'll email you your instructions. Oh, and Maggie...'

'Yes?' she said.

'My name is Max, but my slaves call me master.'

And then he was gone, and Maggie was left sitting on the sofa with the phone in her hand, the sound of her pulse thundering in her ears.

'Oh, my God,' she whispered, wondering what on earth she'd gotten into, and at the same time feeling a compelling flicker of anticipation.

She hurried upstairs and booted up the computer. As Max had promised there was an email waiting for her.

Maggie,

In future you will refer to me as master.

On Sunday I will send a car for you at midday. You will wear a white blouse, loose dark skirt and high-

heeled shoes. You will also wear white underwear and black stockings. You may choose whether to wear a suspender belt or not, although if you make the wrong choice you may expect to be punished. You may wear a suitable coat.

Prior to our meeting you will neatly trim your pubic hair. You will be examined to see that you comply exactly with my instructions. You will stand or sit with your feet parted by eighteen inches.

I look forward to meeting you.

Maggie stared at the screen with a mixture of outrage and excitement; just who the hell did this man think he was? Master indeed! Had she asked for any of this stuff? How dare he assume that she would just do what he said? Trimming her pubic hair? Did he really believe she would just obey and… and… and what?

Angrily she snatched the phone off her desk and dialled Kay's mobile number. This was ludicrous. She didn't care where they were; she needed to speak to Mike.

Just as she was about to press *Call* she read Max's email again and shivered, letting the images trail through her mind; wasn't this exactly what she had always dreamed of?

Chapter Two

The following Sunday morning Maggie stood in front of the mirror in the bathroom and coolly appraised her naked body. She was slim with firm breasts, had a trim waist and shapely hips, and slender legs. At the junction of her thighs nestled a dark triangle of hair, a tight little pelt of curls.

But her mind wasn't just on her appearance. She was mulling over Max's call and the tone of his email.

When the car turned up she would tell the driver or Max or whoever it was driving that there had been a mistake, that she had changed her mind, tell them thanks but no thanks, that she wasn't looking for... for... Maybe she could tell Max that she wanted to talk to him as part of her research, and see how he reacted. He knew she was a writer, so she could ask him for an interview. Maybe she would just go anyway; where was the harm in that? She'd take her mobile, and enough cash to get a cab from wherever it was she found herself.

Still deep in thought she stepped under the shower and let the water wash over her skin. She took the razor off the side of the bath and began to shape the soft curls as Max had instructed. Feeling her excitement slowly begin to build, she let her mind toy with the idea of what it would feel like if she was *really* preparing herself for her master.

It was a compelling thought, and under the torrent Maggie washed and shaved and preened more thoroughly than she had on her wedding day, taking time over every stage.

Of course Max Jordan wouldn't really want to inspect her, she thought, massaging shampoo into her dark hair. It was ludicrous, some kind of mind game to try and rattle her. She soaped her breasts, feeling their warmth and the languid weight of them cupped in her palms, feeling her nipples harden, imagining what it might be like to be made to strip in front of a total stranger. The excitement began to build in her belly, a compelling ache. How would it feel to be in the shower, knowing a stranger was appraising her, watching her every move.

Maggie shivered. It was nearly eleven; another hour and Max would send for her. She threw back her head, relishing the Max of her imagination. If nothing else he had given her a whole new fantasy to enjoy.

Slowly her finger tracked down over her belly, following the path of the razor, Maggie imagining all the while that Max was watching her. Her outer lips were shaved bare now and felt soft and vulnerable. A single finger eased them apart, discovering the moisture already gathering there, her growing excitement clinging to the soft folds of her sex like dew.

With the fingers of her other hand she found her clitoris and circled it, pressing gently down on its sensitive hood. Unable to stop herself she moaned and arched back against the cold tiles; imagining Max Jordan moving closer, his unfathomable eyes fixed on hers; imagining the pleasure in his expression as she touched herself, talking to her, cajoling her, encouraging her to explore her body in the most graphic of terms.

With two fingers deep in her sex, the tight muscles closed around her caress like an eager mouth, sucking them deeper still. Breathing hard Maggie found herself trying to imagine what it would be like to be fucked by the mysterious Max. What would it feel like to have him buried to the hilt inside her? For an instant she imagined an unknown cock driving home, filling her to the brink, making her cry out in a mixture of pleasure and pain as he forced himself deeper than she thought possible.

The first great wave of orgasm took her by surprise, overtaking her like a great flood. Her knees buckled and she slithered to the bottom of the shower, fingers still buried as she thrust onto them, rubbing hard on her clit to milk the last embers of intense heat that had overcome her. And then it was gone and for an instant Maggie reddened furiously, feeling ashamed. How on earth had she got so worked up over a single phone call?

'Maggie?'

She nodded.

'My name is Guido. Max Jordan sent me to pick you up. Are you all ready?'

'Yes, I'm fine,' she said, not quite able to keep the tremor out of her voice, and locking the front door, followed Max's driver towards the black car that sat like a raven at the end of her drive. It was exactly midday and she was dressed as Max had instructed. After all, if she wanted to meet him, for whatever reason, it might be in her best interests to play along.

'Is Max in the car?' she asked the driver. He was dressed in a beautifully tailored black suit that emphasised his broad shoulders and narrow hips. Walking slightly ahead as if guiding her, he swung round and smiled wolfishly.

'Why?' he asked.

It wasn't exactly the response Maggie had expected. 'I, um, just wondered,' she began, and then changed her mind. She would find out in a matter of seconds if her host was there. 'So where are we going?' she did ask.

'Lunch.' As he spoke his eyes moved slowly up her body. 'Mr Jordan is waiting for you.'

Maggie wasn't sure whether she was relieved or disappointed. 'Have you worked for him long?' she asked conversationally. The man opened the rear car door, and taking her hand, helped her inside, waiting while she settled on the cream leather upholstery. His fingers lingered on hers just a little longer than was comfortable, as did his gaze on the elegant curve of her legs.

'Where exactly are we going?' she ventured.

'You ask too many questions.' The driver's gaze did

not falter. 'It will get you into a lot of trouble. I'm taking you to a hotel for lunch, not too far. Don't worry, Max has impeccable taste, in food as well as women, and he is very generous.'

Maggie could hear all kinds of meanings in the words. Generous with his woman as well as his money? That was certainly the implication.

The man smiled as if reading her mind. 'And it pays if you don't forget the rules,' he said as he was about to close the door.

'The rules?' she echoed anxiously.

'Your legs should be open,' he said. Maggie had automatically crossed them upon getting into the car. He leant in and slid a hand between her thighs, and Maggie was so shocked she didn't have time to resist.

'Slaves are meant to be available at all times, legs open, you had better get used to it.'

Maggie felt herself colouring furiously. 'But I'm not a slave,' she countered indignantly.

He smiled, his fingers rubbing her thigh. 'Oh, I think you are,' he said. 'And even if you aren't at the moment, you soon will be. Take my advice; make sure you do exactly as you're told. It pays to learn fast with Max.' And then the door closed and he was climbing into the front seat.

Maggie struggled to regain her composure. In her handbag she had slipped a notebook and pen, the tools of her trade, taken almost like a shield to protect her from Max Jordan. As the car drew away from the kerb she tried to convince herself that she was just playing along to get a decent interview. It would make a great story. Slave master in a modern world. She'd be fine. It wouldn't be the first time she'd felt a little intimidated by her subject, but she knew how to wing it, appear at ease and relaxed even if she wasn't.

The car headed towards the coast, and as Maggie settled she was aware of the driver's eyes in the rear-view mirror, and again she wondered what she'd let herself in for.

Max Jordan watched the car make its way slowly along the quay, then up the hillside towards the hotel. He had booked his usual suite with the sitting room overlooking the harbour. Suitably double-glazed, the French windows that opened onto a sunny terrace not only kept the sea winds out, but all sounds in. The rendezvous was far enough out of town to be private, but not so far as to unnerve his guest.

Max's usual waiter took the champagne from the ice bucket and refilled his glass, while the austere man watched the car's progress. Mike had told him that he considered Maggie a natural, someone who had perhaps suspected she was a submissive for years but fought her natural inclinations.

These were the kind of girls Max liked best – spirited and bright with a fire and passion that if harnessed and trained properly would be a delight for him to enjoy both as slave and companion. It was that combination and his ability to recognise it that ensured his girls always brought the highest prices, whether at auction or in a private sale.

One of the reasons Max loved this suite was the view it afforded him; out beyond the harbour a broad sandbank sheltered the little cove, and beyond that was the open sea. And below, as Maggie climbed the stone steps guided by Guido, he could see her clearly, and it appeared Mike was a better judge than he gave him credit for. He could see the mixed emotions on Maggie's face, in the way she moved. She was nervous, full of expectation and apprehension. He was delighted to see that she was dressed as he had instructed, but wasn't fooled for an instant, for Maggie Howard wasn't obeying him she was humouring him – although it wouldn't be long before she learned the difference.

'Here we are,' said the chauffeur. He stood before the impressive double doors, knocked once and then stepped aside so it was Maggie who waited for permission to enter. As she heard Max Jordan's voice from inside her heart missed a beat. She bit her lip, fingers locked unmoving around the door handle.

'Trust me, it doesn't pay to keep him waiting,' the driver said, and before she knew quite what she was doing, Maggie turned the handle and stepped into the cool room.

Caught in silhouette against a sunlit expanse of glass was a powerfully built man of medium height, probably in his early-fifties, with grey hair, dressed to her surprise in casual trousers and a white shirt, his sleeves neatly rolled up to reveal strong forearms. He had a trimmed beard, heavy but handsome features and a broad mouth. All this Maggie saw and absorbed in an instant. But what she noticed most of all were his eyes – blue-green, glinting, intimidating... yet there was something else, something lurking behind them that was quite impossible to fathom.

'Maggie,' he said in a warm but formal tone. 'How nice to meet you.'

'Max,' she said, with considerably less assurance in her voice. Was she supposed to call him that, or master, and how preposterous an idea was that? She reddened, feeling uncomfortable and unsure in a way she hadn't felt since her teens. Tension crackled in the air between them like the edge of a storm. Maggie shifted her weight, feeling like a lamb waiting for the wolf to decide her fate.

'So,' said Max, taking the champagne bottle from the bucket and pouring a second glass. 'What is it you want? What excuse are you going to use? Are you going to tell me that you're here to interview me, or shall we dispense with the nonsense and the half-truths and the lies, and you tell me what you truly want?' As he spoke he brought the glass to her, all the time his eyes calmly taking in the details of her face and body. It felt as if he was looking into her very soul.

He offered her the champagne and she took it, murmuring her thanks while her heart beat frantically in her chest.

'I don't know, I'm afraid,' she said weakly, almost to herself.

He smiled and gently stroked the line of her jaw. 'I know,' he said.

Maggie trembled, shocked by her reaction to his touch.

'And I do understand, my dear. Drink your champagne then tell me, did you do as I instructed? Did you remove your hair.' His open palm brushed her lower belly so lightly and so fleetingly it was almost like a breath.

'Yes,' she said, eyes downcast, trying to avoid his gaze.

'And what are you wearing under your skirt?'

Maggie felt so self-conscious she thought she might faint. 'White underwear,' she began. 'Although I?'

'Yes, white underwear and what else?' he interrupted. 'Are you wearing suspenders?'

She nodded.

'And you understood my email, that if you made the wrong choice then you would be punished?'

'Yes, but... but surely that was a joke? I mean, you

didn't mean punished, not really.'

He pressed a finger to her lips in a gesture so intimate it took her breath away. 'I'll ask you again, Maggie. Did you understand my email?'

'Yes,' she said, still longing to justify or explain her choice, but he held up his hand to silence her.

'Open the left hand drawer of the bureau and tell me what you find there.'

She looked up at him, eyes bright with fear. 'I don't understand.'

'You will, now do as you're told.'

Uncertainly she walked across the room, opened the drawer and let out a little gasp of panic. Inside was a white envelope with her name written on it, but it wasn't that that made her gasp; it was the leather riding-crop that lay across the envelope.

'Well?' he said, sipping his champagne.

'There's some sort of whip in here, and an envelope.'

'Open the envelope, Maggie,' said Max, from somewhere behind her.

She picked it up, her hands trembling. Inside on a single sheet of paper were the words, *For wearing suspenders your punishment is twenty strokes*.

Maggie swung round as if he'd spoken the words out loud. 'But this isn't fair,' she complained. 'It's ridiculous. How was I to know?'

Max held out his hand to her. 'Bring me the crop, Maggie,' he said, as if she hadn't spoken.

She stiffened, determined to hold her ground. 'How was I to know?' she repeated.

Seconds ticked by, seeming like hours. Max Jordan didn't move, didn't reply, while Maggie's mind raced… and then froze. Wasn't this the very thing she had always imagined? Wasn't it the fantasy that had driven her to a potent climax in the shower? Wasn't this the act of submission that had fuelled countless such fantasies? If she walked away now, if she turned and left, then she might be turning her back on the very thing she longed for.

Maggie took a deep breath to try and still her thoughts, and then very slowly she took the crop from the drawer. For a moment she held it in her hands, trying to imagine what it might feel like to have it crack across her flesh. The idea was both enticing and appalling.

'I'm afraid,' she said, her voice tight with emotion.

'I know, come to me,' he said, and she took one step and then another until they were face to face. 'Now give me the crop,' he said. 'Let me teach you, let me show you what your heart already knows,' and as he spoke Maggie did as she was told, struggling all the while to maintain some shred of composure.

'And now, my little Maggie, you must ask me to punish you,' he said, bending the crop into an arch between his fingers.

Her cheeks flared crimson. 'I must what?' she gasped incredulously.

His voice was low and even and yet incredibly powerful. 'You must ask me, you must say, "master, please punish me".'

'But I can't do that,' she insisted. 'I can't.' All the while she could feel a surge of heat rushing through her and a raw flurry of excitement growing between her legs.

Max shrugged. 'Very well,' he said, and set the crop down on a side table.

Standing there in the silence Maggie wrestled with her fears and her inhibitions, until finally she said, in a voice barely above a whisper, 'Master... please punish me.'

'Very good,' he said as he took her hand, and resistance gone she allowed him to lead her to a large leather armchair. 'Bend over,' he ordered, and she did as she was told. 'Lift your skirt.'

Maggie let out a long slow breath, closing her eyes in shame as she fumbled with the garment, imagining the picture she presented to Max Jordan. Then she leant forward, her hips and bottom in the air, her feet apart to maintain her balance over the chair, her white knickers taut across the rounded contours of her buttocks. She shivered, wondering if she was already wet enough for him to see the moisture seeping through the thin fabric. Her stockings and suspenders framed her bottom as neatly as any picture frame.

She felt Max moving closer and held her breath. She felt his hand brush across the contours of her rear, felt them move between her thighs to the intimacy of her sex, cupping and kneading her through the silky material.

Her colour deepened. He must be able to feel her heat, feel the wetness and the excitement. She moaned and without thinking thrust back against him, some instinctive part of her hoping he would brush her pleasure bud.

'You are a shameless little slut, Maggie,' said Max Jordan. 'You are going to be such a pleasure to train.'

Maggie whimpered with fear and embarrassment as he unhurriedly removed his hand, and the next sensation she felt was the flexible length of the crop being drawn very slowly across her buttocks as if it too were exploring her, letting her know what to expect. Max teased the looped tip across her thighs, between her legs, setting every nerve alight as he caressed her.

'Well, Maggie,' he whispered, 'are you ready?'

She held her breath, then nodded.

'Oh no, my dear, you have to tell me.'

'I... I'm ready,' she whispered uncertainly.

'Then count for me,' he said, and an instant later she felt the crop crack across her waiting flesh. The first stroke was hard enough to make her cry out, her body arching under the blow, a dark pain flooding through her.

'Oh, my God!' she gasped. So this was what it felt like.

'Count,' he snapped.

'One.'

He ran the crop's length under the curve of her buttocks, making her painfully aware of its threatening flexibility – and then just as she began to relax he hit her again, no harder but lower. Maggie shrieked, feeling the breath catch in her throat. It was all she could do to gasp, 'Two,' in a voice she barely recognised as her own.

'Good girl,' he murmured, letting the whip hang in the air for a second. Max watched the way the girl reacted, observing her with the eyes of a true master, watching for signs of her panic and fear, reading and relishing them like a good book. She looked exquisite, bent over the chair, her creamy flesh reddening under his ministrations.

The next stroke was a fraction harder and she cried out again, wondering how hard they would get, whether she would be able to stand the pain, whether having come this far she had made a terrible mistake, and whether she should get away now.

He hit her again and Maggie gasped, 'Four,' between gritted teeth.

Max smiled, feeling the stirring in his groin and more than that, the stirring deep in his soul. He adored hearing his women scream – both with pleasure and with pain He drew back the crop for the fifth stroke; it wouldn't take Maggie long to realise that pleasure and pain were just different sides of the same coin and no more than a heartbeat way.

After the sixth stroke he ran his hand over her glowing backside, stroking and kneading the tender flesh. She was wonderfully wet and he could feel her juices soaking into the thin fabric of her knickers and smell the soft musk of her growing arousal.

This time his finger strayed to rub the throbbing bead of her clitoris. As his fingertip found its mark he could feel her whole body tense and then slowly begin to move against him, seeking a release that, although she was unaware of it, was a very long way off.

Just as she found a rhythm Max stopped and pulled her knickers down to her knees. This time there was no tenderness. He felt her flinch and before she could recover he brought the crop down again across her bare buttocks.

'Ohhh...' she wailed. 'No, please... that hurt, that hurt.'

'How many?' he demanded.

'S-seven,' she sobbed, and he hit her again, her body twisting away. 'Stand still and count, bitch,' he growled.

'Eight,' she gasped. He could hear the tears in her voice but didn't hold back.

'Nine,' she cried out and twisted away again, the weals rising white and then reddening on her creamy skin.

'If you move again I will tie you down,' he warned. 'Perhaps I should tie you anyway...'

Maggie, bent over the chair, trembling furiously, said nothing.

'Well?' he said, drawing the loop of the crop across her legs, the merest touch enough to make her stiffen.

'What do you say? Would you like me to tie you down?'

There was a heady silence, and then she said, 'I don't know.'

He smiled. 'Come, come, my dear, isn't that what you've always dreamed of, to be tied and beaten and used for some faceless man's demands? To be fucked, to suck cock until your mouth fills with spunk, to feel him fucking your cunt, and your arse…?'

Her reply was a muffled sob.

'Well, I am that man, Maggie.' And as he spoke he hit her again.

'Ten!' she cried, her whole frame quivering.

He slipped his free hand between the cheeks of her bottom. Her sex opened like a flower to him and he pressed two fingers deep inside her. She offered no resistance, and as he pulled back he smeared the juice from her sex over the tight little rosebud of her bottom. He felt her tense as he stroked it, and then let his finger move to rub down over the hood of her clit. She let out a little sob of pleasure and he pressed a little harder, dipping back into her sex to lubricate his caress.

'Halfway, Maggie,' he said. 'Well, would you like me to stop?' Silence fell and he felt Maggie wrestling with all the fears and doubts she'd ever had.

After a few moments she said, 'No, master,' in a weak voice, and Max smiled knowingly. He let his hand drop away from the wet confines of her quim and brought back the crop, cracking it across her vulnerable buttocks again. She cried out once more, but this time they both knew something had subtly changed.

'Eleven,' she hissed.

At fifteen he stopped again to caress her beaten bottom. Sixteen and seventeen were relatively gentle, allowing her to settle, the rhythm of the strokes he knew was oddly comforting, and then for the last three he struck hard and fast, the count of twenty lost in a tearful scream.

As soon as he was done he stepped closer to comfort her, touching her face and hair, wet with tears. And then he placed the whip by her cheek. 'It's customary for a slave to thank her master for her punishment and kiss the instrument of her pain.' At once he saw the flash of indignation in her eyes, and smiled; oh yes, Maggie Howard was going to be a real challenge and a real delight.

Slowly, very slowly she looked up at him, her face alight with countless contradictory emotions. 'Thank you,' she whispered, and pressed a fleeting kiss to the punishing leather.

He very delicately drew the loop of the crop across her chin. 'Master,' he prompted.

She bit her lip and then let her gaze fall, cheeks flushed. 'Thank you... master,' she said humbly.

'Now, stand up,' he went on, and she obeyed, then as he turned to refill her champagne glass she moved to pull up her knickers.

'What do you think you're doing?' he barked.

'Getting dressed,' she said, bent over, frozen in the movement.

'Did I tell you to cover yourself up?'

'No, but I thought?'

'No nothing, stay as you are. While you are here with me you are mine. You do as I say; you do not act upon some whim of your own. Do you understand me?'

She nodded.

'Now strip completely.'

'Strip?' she echoed.

He nodded. 'And from now on you will not speak unless I ask you a direct question.'

Very slowly, reluctantly, almost as if her hands belonged to someone else, he watched as Maggie began to unfasten the buttons of her blouse, pulling it back off her shoulders. Beneath was a white lace bra, exquisite against her smooth skin. Next she unfastened her skirt and let it slither to the floor. With her knickers around her knees, Max could see she had done exactly as ordered and neatly trimmed her pubic hair.

She hesitated and looked up at him, eyes full of appeal.

'And the rest,' he insisted, waving a hand towards her.

She unfastened her bra to expose her breasts, the nipples erect, before bending to slip off her panties, suspender and stockings.

Totally naked her eyes filled with tears. She looked so vulnerable standing before him. Max indicated she should turn around, and she did. Her backside was beautifully striped with red weals that were already turning to a delicate shade of purple.

As she turned full circle he handed her the champagne. 'You are very beautiful,' he said.

She blushed and he slipped a hand down between her legs to feel the wet contours of her sex. 'Do you expect me to fuck you today?' he asked.

Her eyes widened. 'I don't know, master,' she said, her brain and tongue struggling to express what she expected.

'There are so many things you don't know, aren't there, little one?' He lifted a hand to cup her breasts, fingers pinching the puckered nipples. She winced, and he pondered with relish just how much more she would wince when he clamped them. From a pocket he took a silk scarf and carefully lifting her hair, he blindfolded her.

Plunged into darkness Maggie stiffened with

apprehension. She waited for what seemed like an eternity, aware of Max moving, picking out a sound on the edge of her hearing, and realised with horror it sounded like metal on metal. Max Jordan took her wrists one at a time and she gasped as she felt cold metal snap shut around them. This was crazy. What was she doing there?

He led her across the room and guided her back onto a chaise longue. He pulled her hands up above her head and secured them to the frame, and then spread her legs, tying each one at the ankle so that her feet were on the floor on either side of the narrow chaise. The rope was slack so she had a little movement. As he worked she thought how strong and insistent he was, but at the same time how oddly gentle his touch, which put her at ease until she realised that bound and blindfolded Max Jordan didn't need to be rough with her – she was his to do with exactly as he wanted.

Once she was secure he ran his hands over her body, lingering on the curves of her breasts and the mound of her sex.

'Do you know how wet you are, my dear?' he drawled. He teased a finger between the lips of her sex, and she knew then, hearing and feeling the wetness.

She whimpered, wondering what on earth was coming next. And then she knew. She felt his breath on her throat and then his teeth nipped her nipples, teasing them into aching hardness before moving down over her belly, slowly down to the heat of her quim.

Surely he wasn't going to... he pulled the outer lips of her sex apart, holding her open while his tongue eased into her, over and over, his mouth and lips joining in sucking and lapping at her pleasure bud. And then there was pain like a bite on the outer labia as he clamped something to it – and then again on the other – the pressure and the nip making her gasp in shock, she cried out and then winced as he pulled her wide open.

She mewled in pain, although her excitement began to build further. She heard him ripping off some sort tape and fixing the clamps back against her belly so that she was totally exposed. His tongue teased and nibbled a counter point to the pain. She pressed her body up against his face, letting him drink her, surrendering totally to his exquisite caress. Despite the clamps she knew she was teetering on the brink of release and so it seemed did Max. As she groaned, eager to reach the point of no return, he pulled away making her instinctively thrust her hips up to him, seeking his tongue.

'Do you want to come, Maggie?' he whispered, and there was no way she could deny it.

'Yes, master,' she sobbed, pressing herself towards the sound of his voice.

'You must ask my permission.'

'Please, master, may I come, please?' she begged, her voice tight with desire and emotion.

His fingers found her clit again, his touch no more than the tiniest brush, the lightest caress, and for an instant Maggie thought she would go mad if he didn't make her climax. Another finger gently pressed at the tight puckering of her anus, teasing and stroking the sensitive nerve-endings, making her writhe and buck against her restraints, and worse still, making her whole body sing. To her horror she felt his lips working towards his fingers, his tongue licking her dark little rosebud with as much skill as seconds earlier he had lapped her clit.

It was so intense, so all consuming that without thinking she begged over and over, not sure whether she was pleading with him to stop or pleading with him to go on.

'That's it, beg me, Maggie,' Max said.

'Please, please make me come,' she pleaded, wriggling against him, now oblivious of the bite of the clamps.

'When?' he goaded.

'Now, please make me come now.'

'I don't think so,' he said cruelly, and pulled away. Maggie tensed in frustration, her body lifting towards him as far as the restraints would allow, but before she could protest any further he pulled off the clamps ands tape. She wailed and gasped as the blood rushed back into the sensitive flesh. Then he took off the blindfold and freed her wrists. She was stunned by his coolness and found it impossible to meet her tormentor's eyes – while between her legs a fire burned so fiercely she was afraid she might be engulfed by it, the temptation to slide a hand down between her thighs almost too much to bear.

Once he had unfastened her ankles, he tipped her chin up to him. 'Look at me, Maggie,' he said, and reluctantly she did as she was told. To her surprise he was smiling. 'I know what you're thinking. Don't touch yourself, for today your body is mine to do with as I please. Here, drink your champagne,' he said, and handed her the glass.

At that moment there was a knock on the door, and Maggie gasped and instinctively bent forward trying to cover her nakedness and her arousal.

'Stay exactly as you are,' Max snapped. 'If you cover yourself I will give you to whoever it is waiting outside.' And then he called, 'Come in!'

The door slowly opened to reveal Guido, his driver, and the uniformed waiter pushing a covered lunch trolley.

The two men set the table by the window as if there was nothing out of the ordinary happening, and once everything was ready Guido remained behind to serve.

Max indicated the table and Maggie stared at him in astonishment, and then accepted the chair Guido held for her.

'Keep you legs open; I want Guido to be able to see you,' Max said as the driver guided the chair back under the table. 'You must learn that as a slave you are available at all times – to whomever I choose.'

As he spoke the driver, lurking behind Maggie, slid a hand over her shoulder and cupped her breast. As she was about to protest he slipped his other hand down to her tummy, two fingers brushing the little triangle of pubic hair.

All the while Max held Maggie's gaze. 'Enough, Guido, thank you,' he said, without letting his eyes leave hers.

Guido's hands moved away, but enmeshed in the look of relief on Maggie's face Max saw a sense of loss too, and smiled to himself. A willing whore was almost more than he could have hoped for so soon after selling Katya.

Chapter Three

Lunch consisted of chicken in a creamy herb sauce that almost melted on the tongue, served with a selection of vegetables and the sweetest new potatoes. Maggie made an effort to concentrate on every mouthful, trying to regain some sense of control.

Guido acted as their waiter, pouring the wine, serving with enviable ease, his expression totally impassive although Maggie sensed his eyes drinking in her nakedness. As they ate Max asked her about her job, her life, and despite Maggie's initial reluctance and more than a little nervousness, she found herself opening up to him in a way she had never expected.

Max Jordan was urbane and charming, his soft Irish accent inviting and almost hypnotic, but not for an instant did Maggie lose sight of her position, or her vulnerability, or the fact that Max's confidence and easy manner masked a dark need to dominate – although what perhaps disturbed her most was that her body responded to it. For all the pain and humiliation she had already experienced at Max Jordan's hands, there was a sense of relief, almost as if she had finally come home.

Dessert, fresh strawberries and cream, was followed by coffee, and then from across the table Max said in that wonderfully melodious tone, 'A good slave understands her place and is happy there. Her role is to anticipate her master's every wish and obey his every command.'

Maggie reddened. It was the first time whilst eating that the conversation had returned to the subject of slavery, although it wasn't far from her mind. She longed to ask him how he had become a master and why, but despite her curiosity and the supposed article she was supposed to be writing, she couldn't quite bring herself to voice the question.

Max signalled to Guido, who set the two coffee cups down side by side on the tabletop. 'You will serve me, Maggie, my coffee and a brandy,' he ordered.

Maggie nodded and he raised an eyebrow, quite clearly expecting something more.

'Yes, master,' she said hastily, the words sounding somewhat silly and clumsy.

He smiled as her colour intensified. 'And then you

will get a taste of what it feels like to be a man's possession. For the rest of the time you are here you'll kneel at my feet, like a good slave, knees parted, back straight. Some masters will want you to keep your hands behind your head or neck, but I prefer them held neatly behind your back. You will sit like that until and unless I instruct you to do otherwise.'

Maggie swallowed heavily.

'Do you understand me?' he pressed.

Her gaze lowered. 'Yes, master,' she said meekly.

'Stand up,' he snapped, the warmth leaving his voice. 'I will have my coffee on the terrace.' Then without another word he stood and headed outside.

Maggie looked at the coffee cups, and then anxiously at Guido, whose face remained as resolutely impassive as ever.

'White, milk not cream, no sugar,' he said as her discomfort grew, taking the second cup for himself and adding cream.

He passed a tray to her with a brandy glass on it.

'Thank you,' she said nervously, arranging the cup next to the glass.

'No need to thank me, slave,' Guido said. 'I'm sure we'll be able to find a way to work your debt off later.'

Maggie stiffened, and would have asked him exactly what he meant if she hadn't caught sight of Max waiting outside for her. 'I've already told you,' Guido said, 'it doesn't pay to keep him waiting.'

Maggie went out through the French windows. The terrace was sheltered, a perfect suntrap, and to her relief extremely private.

Max smiled. 'Thank you, slave,' he said, taking the coffee and brandy.

The light breeze whipped at her hair, making her shiver both with cold and anticipation. She set the tray down on the table beside his chair, and then more reluctantly knelt down beside him on the warm deck. Max waited until she was settled and then ran a hand over her shoulders and hair, leaning forward to cup a breast and squeeze her nipples.

'Slaves aren't just marked by their obedience, little one,' he told her. 'Most wear a mark to show their position, to show who they belong to.'

From the hotel room Guido appeared carrying a flat velvet pouch. Maggie looked up with a mixture of curiosity and surprise.

'Did I tell you to look at him?' Max barked. 'Or move?'

'No, master,' she said quickly.

Max pinched her nipple, making her wince and simper.

'Get up,' he ordered. 'If you become a slave you don't need to think or decide what to do; others will make decisions for you. You have no need to be curious at what things are, because trust me, what is yours will come to you.'

They stood close, face to face, Maggie with her eyes still demurely downcast, trying hard to stop the little tremble that flickered though her body like an anarchic pulse. She wanted to protest, tell him that she wasn't anyone's slave, and that she had no intention of becoming one of his slaves, but something made her hesitate.

Was it a fear that if she said the words aloud then he would send her away? Would he reject her? Although she found it hard to admit to herself, if that happened she would be consumed with regret and would never have or taste the heady secrets this strange liaison promised.

'When you stand you will have your hands behind

your back, legs apart.'

Maggie nodded and took a deep breath to try and still her racing pulse, so caught up in calming herself that what Max did next took her totally by surprise. Drawing back his hand he slapped her breast, catching it squarely on the side, making her gasp in shock, and then he struck the other one, catching the nipple. She bit her lip and looked up at him in astonishment.

'Count,' he said flatly.

'One...' she responded hastily.

He struck again, harder.

'T-two.' What was she doing, letting him do this? It seemed even more bizarre than letting him take a crop to her bottom. The sensation of heat and pain spread through her torso. 'Th-three!'

The forth blow made her shriek and twist away from him. 'Guido!' he barked, and the servant handed him a black ribbon with a white ball secured halfway along it. He smiled, eyes narrowing. 'Do you know what this is, my dear?' he asked.

Maggie shook her head. 'No, master, I don't,' she said honestly.

'It's a ball-gag,' he told her. 'Let me show you how it works. Open you mouth.'

The ball sat uncomfortably between and behind her teeth, holding her mouth wide open and making swallowing difficult. Despite her best efforts a trickle of saliva ran down her chin. She looked at Max in horror, who smiled again, drew back his hand and struck her breast harder still. The gag successfully muffled her shriek.

'We can't go disturbing our fellow guests, now can we?' he said, slapping her again. 'And if you move again, Maggie, I'll string you up on the railings.

After twenty he stopped and she hoped he would

remove the gag – but no. Instead he took the velvet bag from his driver and from inside produced a black leather collar set with a band of stainless steel. There were three rings set into the steel, and the collar was hinged at the back and fastened with a little padlock, which was stamped with what looked like an heraldic device. As Maggie stared she realised the emblem consisted of the letters M and J.

'Would you like to try it on?' he said.

Maggie shivered, unable to work out the right answer; not that it sounded like a genuine question, and with the ball-gag in place her answer would be restricted to nodding or shaking her head.

'And I did say try,' he said, tipping her face up to his. 'You will only be expected to wear a collar on a more permanent basis if you accept the terms of my contract, Maggie. Well?'

He held the collar out towards her and she stepped closer, afraid to think for fear of where those thoughts might lead her. Max fed the collar around her throat, snapped it closed and fastened the lock. It fitted snugly.

'You look magnificent,' he said, stepping back to admire her, his eyes studying her face, the ball-gag wet with saliva, the collar and then the glowing orbs of her breasts.

'Good,' he nodded, as if speaking to himself, his gaze moving lower still. She felt like a prize animal and tried not to let a growing sense of panic or unnerving desire overwhelm her. It wasn't that the collar was uncomfortable, it was what it and the gag symbolised. Surrender, silence, obedience – and a terrifying glimpse of a trust of the most fundamental kind, that she realised would have to grow if she stepped into this ring of fire with Max Jordan. She would quite literally have to trust him with her mind, her body and her soul.

He sat down and opened his legs. 'Come here and lay across my knees,' he told her, and without a word, still reeling from the snap of the collar, Maggie did as she was told. For a moment she lay totally still, listening to her own heartbeat, feeling the press of his trousers against the sensitive glow of her skin, trying to find a place where she felt balanced, and then Max said, 'You are disobedient and wilful, and yet I know that in your chest beats the heart of a true slave, Maggie. I can feel it, I can see it.'

How could he be so certain when she was so unsure?

He stroked her buttocks, working his fingers against the welts left by the crop.

'I can teach you, Maggie. I can show you.' She closed her eyes, the glow simmering before lunch still there between her legs, hidden a little by fear but nevertheless within an instant of rekindling. 'But you have to learn to obey me. Do you understand?'

'Hmmm,' she mumbled through the gag, wondering why he hadn't removed it, and then she found out why. His hand exploded across her bottom making her convulse, and as she shrieked in horror Max drew her arm behind her back and spanked her again.

She sobbed and shook her head desperately, but his hand found the mark again. Tears coursed down her face and at the same time, and to her shame, the glow in the pit of her stomach began to build again.

Four more spanks were delivered and then he pressed two fingers into her sex, roughly, and her hips lifted to give him access, desperate for his caress. She heard him laugh with pleasure, and no longer cared.

Pushing her off his lap she rolled wearily onto the wooden decking. 'Get up on all fours, you little bitch,' he snapped, and without a second thought Maggie did as she was told, and was utterly shocked to feel his rampant cock drive into the wet confines of her cunt, filling her, making her gasp with shame and delight. She sobbed as he penetrated her, both at the ferocity of his entry and at the relief and joy of finally feeling his erection buried deep inside her.

As he fucked her she met him stroke for stroke, gasping behind the gag as his hands sought her nipples, twisting and tormenting them before moving down to her clit, nipping and stroking the engorged bud until she felt the roaring wave of orgasm about to wash her away.

'You may come,' he panted in her ear, his weight on her back, and she was lost, borne up, carried away by the most intense sensations she had ever experienced. She cried out again and again as he drilled deeper still, riding the tightening of her sex cocooning him, and she knew he was with her every step of the way, driving deep, arching and crying out as the wave overtook him too.

When they were done Maggie turned and slumped into his arms, sated, shivering and raw with emotion.

'You're not done yet, little one,' he said, and she stared at him in weary bewilderment. He undid the ball-gag. 'A good slave always cleans her master. With your mouth,' he added, running a finger around her lips. 'After I have taken my pleasure, you will clean me.'

She looked down at his cock. Even spent it was impressive, long and thick with a smooth helmet, wet and glistening with their combined juices.

'Well?' he said, and without complaint Maggie knelt over him and took his cock into her mouth, tasting their salty flavours. He sighed and stroked her hair, and after a few minutes he gently he pulled her away and kissed her on the lips.

'Come with me,' he said, and together they rose. 'A good slave always walks two paces behind her master,' he informed her.

Maggie did as she was told, trying to ignore the avaricious glint in Guido's eyes as he stood by the door, watching her. He gave her the barest of smiles, and she couldn't contain an uneasy shudder.

Guido let the smile linger on his lips. He had been with Max for over two years as valet and driver, and in return Max was teaching him all he knew. Another couple of months and he would be on his way and begin his own stable. Maybe he'd make a bid for Maggie when she stepped up on the block; it would be nice to start with one of his master's girls as a yardstick. She was certainly extremely appealing, headstrong and bright, but even he could sense that under that apparent self-confidence and independence she had a strong desire to please, to be wanted, to be owned.

The way she had writhed and sobbed under Max's ministrations had truly been a delight. Guido replayed in his mind the way the girl waited on all fours to be fucked. There was no way she faked any of that.

He straightened his tie, already relishing the prospect of the drive home.

'And when dressed, in public,' Max continued as they stepped back into his suite, 'a good slave will always look and behave impeccably, like a lady; elegant with appropriate clothes, good shoes, subtle make-up and perfume. My slaves are always well presented.

'My main interest has always been in the initial training of suitable girls – in recognising those who will make good slaves and interesting companions. I train them in the basics and then sell them on. We have regular auctions. There is always a lot of interest in my girls.'

'Sell them?' Maggie echoed, unable to contain herself.

Max smiled, apparently forgiving her for speaking without permission.

'Yes, sometimes we sell privately but for the most part we auction off our spare stock, or those we're tired of, or whatever. Besides that we often have auctions where slaves are sold for just a night or a weekend.'

Maggie felt her colour draining. He was talking about his slaves as if they were animals, and worse still, as she considered what he said, was the realisation that somewhere – just below the surface of the life she knew – was a culture where this kind of behaviour went on.

The idea not only unnerved her but also, she realised, excited her. Max took her hand and led her into the bedroom.

'Lie on your back on the bed,' he told her. 'Legs parted.'

Maggie stared at him in disbelief, and then at the four-poster bed that dominated the room. Surely he couldn't be ready for more – he'd only just spent.

'Come along, there is no place for coyness now, Maggie,' he snapped, his mood volatile. 'You will follow my instructions instantly and to the letter. Now!'

She looked at him uncertainly, heart beating fast, and then did as she was told, closing her eyes to block out the images that filled her head.

'Very nice,' he said. 'Now hold yourself open so I can examine you.'

Maggie froze... examine her?

'What are you waiting for?' he growled.

'I can't,' Maggie whispered. 'Please, I... I can't.'

The silence and the seconds ticked slowly by, and then Max said. 'For every minute you keep me waiting I will add six strokes of the crop to your punishment.

Now open your cunt for me.'

Maggie let her fingers trail down over her belly, eyes tightly closed. This was ludicrous. Why should she obey him? But then taking a deep breath she let her fingers slip between the outer lips of her sex, warm and wet with excitement. She opened herself a little, praying the gesture would be enough.

'Wider,' he snapped.

Maggie did as she was told, feeling herself flush scarlet. It wouldn't have been so bad if Max touched her, but he didn't, he was just watching and waiting.

'Guido, come in here,' he eventually called, and Maggie cringed with shame, wanting to pull her fingers away and close her legs. 'Stay as you are,' Max ordered, anticipating her reaction. 'Did I tell you to move?'

'N-no, master,' she stammered.

'What do you think?' Max said conversationally, and Maggie knew he wasn't talking to her.

Guido mumbled something and she felt him moving closer, felt his eyes and breath on her.

'Get up on all fours so Guido can have a better look at you,' Max ordered, and she stiffened, feeling her stomach tighten with shame and apprehension.

The driver ran his hands over her buttocks and hips, letting his fingers stray down to her sex, thrusting, exploring, probing inside her with none of the finesse employed by Max Jordan.

'Nice and tight,' he observed, as her sex instinctively tightened around him.

'Indeed... indeed,' Max concurred, and embarrassed beyond all measure Maggie let her head fall to the mattress, feeling she would die of shame. Guido parted her further and pushed another finger inside, her flinch doing nothing to halt his invasive touch.

'Help yourself,' said Max. 'I'm going down to the bar

for a drink. You can do whatever you like, just don't fuck her.'

Alone with the driver Maggie's heart pounded furiously; ridiculous though it was she already held some trust for Max Jordan, but not this other man. He removed his fingers, and she felt his tongue lapping the backs of her thighs and then wriggle into her sex. She gasped at the intensity and intimacy of the touch, his nose nudging her puckered rear entrance as he devoured her.

She felt shamefully uncomfortable, but there were the first flickers of renewed pleasure too. She cringed; had her body no shame at all? Guido slid a finger up to caress her clit, and she moaned as he brushed the tight little peak. It was all the encouragement he needed. He began to lap at her quim and then worked further up along the sensitive bridge of flesh between her sex and the forbidden entrance above. Maggie whined in horror, trying to wriggle away from him, and then gasped as his tongue brushed over her anus, lapping and teasing.

'Oh!' she gasped. 'No, please don't. Oh!' But her protests seemed to make his tongue work all the more diligently while his fingers teased her pleasure bud.

'Please don't... please don't,' she whispered, his tongue driving her mad with need. It felt wonderful and awful at the same time.

'Enough, Guido,' said a familiar voice. 'We can't have Miss Howard enjoying herself too much, now can we?'

The driver pulled away, leaving Maggie hanging, her sex wet and ready for more, her bottom slick with his saliva.

'Look at you, you filthy little whore,' Max Jordan sniggered, and without prelude he pressed a finger into the tight confines of her rectum. Maggie cried out in shock, her body fighting the invasion.

'Nice and tight,' he concluded. 'Maybe a little too tight at the moment for what I have in mind, but we can cure that. Have you ever been fucked in the arse, Maggie?'

'No,' she gasped in horror, aware that her body was clutching his intrusive digit. Another finger slipped into her sex, the fullness and the intense sensations making her feel heady.

'I like to bugger my slaves,' he mused. 'It's my own special place, somewhere that's mine and mine alone – no other man is allowed to fuck you there. They can fuck your cunt, fuck your mouth, fuck your tits, but your arse is mine.'

Maggie shivered; it seemed appalling and unnerving that such a sophisticated man could speak so crudely about her body, and his desires and plans to use and abuse it. His fingers left her.

'I think that is enough for now,' he said, as casually as if they were taking an afternoon stroll. 'Get up.'

A little unsteadily, Maggie got to her feet.

'Now,' he said, 'before we go any further...' Maggie looked up at him expectantly, and saw the intent in his eyes. 'Every slave I take on must sign a contract.'

'A contract?' she echoed uncertainly.

'Be quiet. I have warned you about speaking so freely. I take no one on without a contract, and once it is signed you are committed to it. I consider it a legally binding contract and so should you. And you also have to understand that at the end of your training, I will sell you.'

Despite everything that had happened Maggie found this revelation unbelievable. It was preposterous, some sort of a joke. No one in their right mind signed themselves away under someone else's rule.

Max continued. 'I am a firm master, but fair,' he told her. 'I understand what you need but I won't rush you to achieve it.'

Maggie squashed the look of derision that threatened. What man ever really knew what a girl wanted?

He raised an eyebrow, as if anticipating a question, and when none came he continued. 'Would you like to see the contract?'

Maggie was intrigued. 'Yes, master,' she said, and Max made a gesture towards Guido, who handed him a briefcase from which he produced a single sheet of paper and handed it to her.

'There we are, my dear,' he said. 'The contract.'

Slowly she began to read. 'I, Maggie Howard, hereafter referred to as the slave, do offer myself to Max Jordan, hereafter known as my master, for his pleasure in a BDSM relationship, as defined in detail as follows...'

Maggie glanced uncertainly at Max, then at Guido, then back at the document in her trembling hands.

'The slave is fully aware that her master is a strict dominant, and that she is a willing slave to be used for his desired pleasures. The slave expects the domination of her master and is willing to endure any and all punishments deemed appropriate by him.

'I hereby grant permission to my master to dispense any punishment he may deem appropriate to the slave totally for his enjoyment and the pleasure of hearing the slave request his mercy.

'The slave will be under her master's complete and total control and will immediately obey and comply with any order or instruction given to her with the full joy of knowing she is his property and his to use however he chooses. If the slave displeases or disobeys her master in any way she expects to endure any punishment he so chooses as necessary for her inappropriate actions.

'The slave also agrees not to make any change in her physical appearance without the prior approval of her master.

'The slave agrees to full participation in any and all activities her master desires as she does not know the extent of her limits with him at this point and desires to learn how complete is her submission to him.

After thorough training is completed the slave will be sold to the highest bidder.

Maggie reddened furiously and felt her pulse increase as she finished reading. Then she read it again, more slowly this time, not trusting herself to look up and meet Max Jordan's eyes.

It gave her an odd feeling deep in her stomach. In her imagination the scenario of being owned and used and shown off was hugely exciting, but the reality? She had no intention of signing herself away. What on earth did the man take her for? She looked at him levelly. 'I am expected to sign this?' she said.

'No, there is no expectation on my part. The choice is entirely yours, Maggie. But before you dismiss the idea and walk away, let me tell you something about yourself. Even if you don't sign you will never be free. Today you've caught a brief glimpse of those things that have haunted your dreams, maybe even your nightmares, for a long, long time.'

She looked away; he was far too close to the truth for it to feel comfortable. But Max hadn't finished.

'And I know, Maggie, because I see it in your eyes. I know from my own experience that you can never escape those desires that are in your mind.' His tone changed. 'But maybe you've already got enough for your article. Isn't that what you came for?'

Maggie nodded.

'Well, in that case you are free to go.' Her dismissal was so perfunctory it took her by complete surprise. Max pulled a key ring from his pocket, beckoned her closer and removed the collar, which Guido immediately returned to its black velvet bag.

She extended a hand to give him the contract back, but Max waved it away. 'Take it with you,' he said. 'I wouldn't have expected you to sign it here and now anyway. You need to be sure you understand all the implications of something so momentous, but remember you must sign it before your training begins.'

Maggie smiled. 'Thank you,' she said, and went to retrieve her clothes. She had no intention whatsoever of signing his stupid contract. The idea was ridiculous. Utterly ridiculous.

'You have to understand, Maggie,' he went on as she dressed, 'that you will never win and you will never escape.'

She wondered what he meant, and then realised with a growing sense of unease that it was some kind of a threat – except that the threat was from inside her, not from Max Jordan.

'Thank you for lunch,' she said, as casually as she could manage.

He smiled confidently. 'Guido, show the young lady to the bathroom.'

When Maggie re-emerged not more than half an hour later, showered and dressed, the suite was empty, all evidence of lunch and of Max Jordan's presence gone. All that remained was Guido – standing by the door waiting to drive her home, his peaked cap resting lazily between his fingers.

'Well, well, well,' he said with a sly grin. 'Here we

are again, Miss Howard. How does it feel now you know what Max Jordan has to offer you?'

Maggie tried to smile with conviction. 'It feels just fine, thank you. I don't want what Mr Jordan has to offer, though. I've seen enough, and I don't want any part of it.'

Guido shook his head, and Maggie wondered if the lie was as obvious to him as it was to her.

'But I am interested in what makes a man like him tick,' she continued; after all, she reasoned, if there really was an article in it, she could do with a bit more background material.

'You should have asked him, then,' said Guido, standing to one side to allow her to pass. 'I'm sure Max would have told you anything you wanted to know.' He paused as Maggie drew level with him. 'And so would I. For a price, of course.'

'What does that mean, exactly?' she demanded.

'Oh, come on, Maggie, don't be so naïve,' he said with mock disappointment, tutting loudly. 'I tell you something and then you pay for it in kind.'

Maggie stared at him indignantly, and without thinking swung her arm to slap his face. But he was too quick for her and caught her wrist in a vicelike grip that made her wince with pain.

'He told me you could be fiery,' Guido mused, chuckling throatily, his smile never faltering. 'A good judge of character, is Max Jordan.'

'Which is more than can be said for you,' snapped Maggie, angrily jerking her hand away from him.

Guido smiled. 'If you would like to wait outside I'll bring the car to the front of the hotel,' he said with infuriating assuredness.

Chapter Four

'Where are we now?' Maggie asked, leaning forward in the back seat of the car and looking out at the passing countryside, trying hard to spot a familiar landmark. To her complete surprise, after the events of the afternoon, she had drifted off to sleep on the drive home. Feeling slightly foolish she repeated her question. 'Where are we, Guido?'

She caught the driver's eye in the rear-view mirror. He smiled lazily. 'Don't worry, it's not far now,' he said. 'Why don't you just sit back and enjoy the ride. I'll let you know when we get there.'

Something about his tone made her uneasy. 'But I don't recognise this road,' she said, trying to keep the anxiety out of her voice. 'How far are we from Richwell?'

He laughed. 'I've already told you, relax. This is the scenic route. There's no rush, is there?'

Making an effort not to look or sound flustered, Maggie turned her attention back to the view outside the car. It was a beautiful evening. The early summer sun was slowly sinking in the west, daubing the undulating landscape with a mellow golden light. Ahead of them the road unfolded like a ribbon, and Maggie looked for some clue as to where they might be, the tension in her stomach building. She had no idea where they were or where they were heading, and just as she was about to ask again the car slowed and they crossed a narrow wooden bridge that led off the road and through a copse of trees.

Maggie didn't like this. On the road they may well have been taking a scenic route home she wasn't familiar with, but this was little more than a dirt track leading to she knew not where.

The car was travelling more slowly now, rising and falling over the uneven surface.

'Guido, what's going on?' she asked anxiously. 'Where are we? You're supposed to be taking me home.'

'Don't worry,' Guido said, his wolfish smile caught in the mirror. 'I thought you wanted to know how it felt to be a slave? Isn't that why you met Max today, to get your hands on a little background information? Well, this is lesson two.'

'I wanted to know about Max Jordan,' she began, humouring him.

'I've already told you that I'm prepared to tell you everything you need to know,' he said, guiding the car into a clearing and switching off the ignition. 'I've told you the deal, it's just that now I've upped the stakes a little.' He indicated the narrow track that led back to the road. 'How about it, Maggie?' he said, the grin holding. 'A ride for a ride. Part of your continuing education, or maybe a little payment on account.'

Maggie forced a smile, trying to mask her trepidation. 'Let's go back, Guido,' she suggested. 'I can pay you something, but not much,' she began. 'Perhaps we could negotiate?'

'You know that isn't what I mean,' he sneered angrily, cutting her short. 'I don't want or need your money.'

Maggie said nothing; she already knew what the deal was. Hadn't he told her as she left the hotel?

'So, I'm going to have the rest of what I sampled this afternoon.' He licked his lips. 'You taste really good.' Maggie reddened and he chuckled. 'Come on, don't tell me you didn't enjoy it. I could feel the way you were moving under my tongue and my fingers. There was no lie there, you were close.'

Maggie shivered. 'Guido, please...' she began.

'No more talk, just get out of the car.' His tone hardened. 'I can take what I want or you can give it to me – simple as that. It's up to you.'

Maggie looked left and right through the trees. They were miles from anywhere. There was no point in running. There was nowhere to hide. What choice did she have? And besides, wasn't there some tiny part of her, some part she would never admit to, that was excited by the idea that the man wanted her so much he would jeopardise his job to have her? Hadn't she relished the humiliation of being given to him at the hotel, to play with just as he wanted? Maggie fought to silence the rogue thoughts.

'This is ridiculous,' she said instead. 'Take me home. I won't say anything about this to Max.'

Guido laughed. 'You really think he'd mind? You have to understand, Maggie, that slaves are mere possessions, toys to be used. I thought Max had made that clear to you.'

She stared at him, trying to gather her thoughts. What could she do other than try and talk him out of whatever obscene plan lurked behind those dark eyes?

'Get out of the car,' he said, his tone icy. But Maggie didn't move, and his expression hardened. 'Now!' he spat. 'And take your skirt off.'

Maggie bit her lip, considering her options. What was she going to do? She guessed Guido would be a lot less controlled than Max, and decided that her best course of action was to humour him.

Slowly, very slowly, heart pounding in her chest, Maggie slipped across the seat and did as she was told, trying to formulate an alternative while unzipping her blue skirt and letting it drop to the grass. Underneath she was wearing the white underwear and stockings and suspenders stipulated by Max Jordan.

Guido's eyes moved hungrily over her body. 'Max was right, you are a natural,' he said, and Maggie reddened under his undisguised lust.

'Guido, please,' she began, wondering if she could appeal to his better nature. But he was having none of it, and instead he lunged and cupped her sex through the thin fabric of her panties, fingers tightening, squeezing hard enough to make her whimper.

'I want this,' he growled, 'and I intend to have it. And as I said, Maggie, either you give it to me or I'll take it.'

He looked her up down as if relishing her growing apprehension. 'Now I want you to strip for me, or would you prefer me to rip your clothes off?'

Without another word Maggie slipped off her knickers and undid her suspender belt, uncomfortably aware of his intrusive stare. Being outside in the woods made her feel doubly exposed, doubly vulnerable.

As she straightened up from removing her stockings Guido, annoyed at the delay, roughly unfastened her blouse, pushed up her bra and grabbed a breast in each hand, dragging her tight against him, his kisses hard and hungry while his hands squeezed the tender flesh until she cried out into his mouth. His cruel touch made her reel with a terrible sense of fear and resignation and also, and to her abject horror, sexual hunger. Was this what slavery and submission truly meant? Slavery to your own terrible desires?

'Take off the rest of your things and bend over the car bonnet,' he said. 'And spread your legs wide so I can see exactly what I'm getting.' He pushed her away towards the waiting vehicle.

Maggie closed her eyes, trembling, going through the motions while her mind was in turmoil. How had it come to this? Naked, shivering and afraid she settled down over the broad polished black bonnet without another word, her forearms supporting her while Guido explored her body, her back, her breasts, her buttocks; no place was spared his crude examination, his invasive fingers investigating the welts Max had striped her with. Then just as she began to find some sense of composure, some safe inner space, he kicked her feet further apart, leaving her even more vulnerable to his explorations.

'Give me your wrists, here,' he snapped. 'Put them behind your back.' She closed her eyes, knowing that some part of her had already surrendered.

Helpless, with her cheek pressed against the warm bodywork, Guido jerked her arms back and tied them together at the wrist with a length of cord.

'Well, well, well,' he said, breathing hard. 'The little madam out to do some research. Did you think it would bring you this far?'

She held her breath, too afraid to reply.

He caught hold of her hair and jerked her head back. 'Well, what have you to say for yourself? There's no Max here now to protect you, no safety net. You're all mine. Did I tell you that Max is training me to be a master too? I've learnt a lot from him, but I've always known in my heart what really turns me on; a delicious girl fighting and struggling against me, crying out, begging for mercy, writhing and sweating... that's what excites me.'

Maggie froze, then heard Guido spitting, felt his fingers work the saliva into her quim and then felt the hard press of his cock probing the lips of her sex, before he plunged into her with one smooth penetration.

The invasion took her breath away, his cock large and stout. She wailed with shock and without thinking begged him to stop. 'Please, you're hurting me,' she sobbed, knowing full well that's what Guido wanted to hear, and secretly experiencing the reawakening of her carnal desires. As she struggled beneath him he pushed deeper still, holding her hips to pull her back onto his rampant erection.

'Please, Guido, no please,' she rambled, even though her treacherous body was responding to him. And Max's driver was already beyond any discussion, turning back or reasoning. He locked his fingers tight in her hair, pulling her up to him, dragging her off the car, bending her back like an archer's bow, her exposed breasts thrusting forward.

As he rutted into her again and again his free hand mauled her breasts and twisted her nipples. Maggie cried out in pain and shock, while deep inside she felt her own dark passion building inexorably, ashamed of what she was feeling. How could such an animal excite her so much? How was it that this violation, this abuse of her body by a man who was practically a stranger, was the very thing that ignited the fires in the pit of her stomach? Maggie was ashamed of herself, even more than she loathed Guido.

He grunted like an animal, driving on and on, excited by her physical and verbal reactions. As he got closer to the point of no return he pulled her fully back against his body and clamped his arms around her waist, biting her neck and lapping her hot flesh.

'You love this, don't you, you dirty little bitch?' he growled between clenched teeth.

Maggie said nothing, trying desperately to retain some last shred of self-control.

'Tell me,' he snapped. 'You like to feel a cock deep in your cunt, don't you? Don't you? Tell me.'

He twisted his fingers tight in her hair and jerked her

head back, making her shriek in pain.

'Yes!' she gasped, horrified to hear herself admit it.

'Yes what?' he pressed. 'What is it you like, you dirty little bitch?'

Maggie shivered as he drove deeper still, emphasising his questioning, making her cry out again as his cock filled her. 'T-to feel a cock d-deep inside me,' she stammered, writhing with pleasure and shame. His fingers tightened in her hair and around her nipple and she squealed. 'Deep in my cunt!' And Maggie knew it was true. She wanted him to use her, just as she had wanted Max to use her. She wanted Guido to take her over the edge into oblivion, and instinctively began to move against him, grinding her arse back into his groin, tipping her hips so that his body angled perfectly against hers.

'What do you want me to do then, Maggie?' Guido growled in her ear, as if sensing the change in her.

'I... I want you to fuck me,' she gasped. 'Please, fuck me. Make me come. Please... please, Guido.'

As she begged he snorted derisively, pulled out of her and pushed her down onto the grass. 'On your knees,' he growled, and Maggie, sobbing with frustration, did as she was told, stumbling with her hands tied, knees parted to maintain her balance.

Guido leered down at her, stroking her hair back off her damp brow, running his fingers over her breasts and lips and throat. And then he arrogantly brushed her chin and cheeks with his rigid shaft. It was slippery and smelt of her own excitement, then grabbing her hair again he stroked the bulbous tip across her lips, and then fed it deep into her mouth.

The taste and smell of him suffused her senses; the heady mixture of aroused male musk mixed with the flavours of her own body was almost more than she could bear. Her lips were slick with his pre-cum and more than anything she wished her hands were free so she could touch herself and him. Her whole body was screaming for release.

Guido towered above her, dominant and full of lust, obviously relishing the way her tongue and lips worked over the head of his cock, enjoying the special attention as the kneeling girl submissively lapped and sucked his shaft deep into her mouth. Maggie could feel his pleasure building along with her own. She heard him grunt, felt the tension increasing in his balls and braced herself for the great flood of seed to fill her mouth.

Guido thrust once, twice, and for a moment she was convinced he was going to ejaculate and make her drink his seed, but then at the very last second he pulled out, dragging her head back and splashed her face and breasts and cleavage with this warm spunk. She gasped as it splattered on her flesh.

He grinned triumphantly down at her, catching his breath. 'Now you look like a whore – and you certainly act like one.'

Maggie felt so ashamed she wanted to die, but it seemed her torture wasn't over yet. Guido, his cock still wet and slick with combined juices, dragged her to her feet and back over the bonnet of the car, on her back this time, and to her horror he began to lap up the trail of warm semen that clung to her body, licking and sucking her face and breasts. Seeing the shock on her face he smiled and kissed her, pushing his tongue, slick with spunk, deep into her mouth.

Maggie shuddered and tried to roll her head to one side, tried to push him away. But Guido merely laughed and continued to lick her, her face and her ears, sucking her nipples into his mouth, biting and nipping. Maggie gasped and began to moan, beginning to lose it again, overcome by so many sensations and needs that threatened to engulf her.

But still there was no reprieve. Gradually Guido was working lower, spreading her legs until there was no part of her that was not exposed to his fingers and his lips.

'You taste wonderful,' the driver drooled, plunging his tongue deep inside her and then lapping at her quim like a hungry dog.

Maggie cried out, part of her horrified by the exposure, the other half afraid that he might stop. Finally he sank down amongst the grass and the leaves beneath the trees, and Maggie gasped as he lifted her bodily and set her legs over his shoulders, his tongue moving between her thighs, devouring her sex. He slavered against her and then, just when she thought she would go mad with desire, he located her clitoris.

Maggie cried out with relief and pleasure. Instinctively her hips thrust to meet the driver's tongue, oblivious to everything but the bliss building deep inside. He slid a finger into her quim and another lodged just inside the puckered bud of her bottom. She groaned and writhed against his touch; Guido surely had to be Max Jordan's star pupil.

She closed her eyes tight, all rational thoughts vanishing into the abyss as wave after wave of pleasure rolled over her, but then he pulled away and Maggie whimpered with frustration.

'Come on then, ask me, I want to hear you beg,' he goaded, his tone thick with desire. 'Beg me, bitch. Beg me for what you want.'

'Oh,' Maggie sobbed, 'please don't stop now, Guido, please don't stop. I'm so close, lick me... suck me... please. Please make me come.'

Guido's tongue brushed across her pleasure bud.

Maggie groaned again, lifting her hips. He lapped a little harder, and it was almost more than she could bear.

'Please, please,' she sobbed, any last shred of pride lost in the hungry pit of desire as he circled the little peak with the tip of his tongue. For an instant Maggie thought she might go mad and then the wave broke over her.

'I'm going to come!' she shrieked. 'I'm going to... oh... oh!' She shuddered, rolling from side to side, her sex grinding into his face. And as she peaked she felt him rise and sink his rejuvenated cock deep, deep into her sex. Her body closed around him and he followed her into oblivion seconds later, throwing back his head and grunting like a wild animal as he drove his cock into her.

And then finally they were both still and all Maggie could hear was their ragged breathing, the pound of her pulse and the rustling of the trees.

As the car made its slow way back down the uneven track, Max Jordan stepped out from behind the shelter of a tree and watched the red taillights disappear into the distance. Guido was somewhat crude in his technique, but Maggie Howard was far better than he had hoped for.

He walked slowly back to his own car considering the way the day had gone and what he had just witnessed. He smiled; he was going to enjoy training this one.

Maggie sat up in bed, her thoughts racing. The room was dark except for a ribbon of moonlight falling through the open curtains and settling across her duvet. It had to have been a dream, didn't it? A dream? More like a nightmare!

She switched on the bedside light, and there on the

bedside cabinet was Max Jordan's contract. She closed her eyes, dropped her head into her hands for few seconds and then with a growing sense of determination got out of bed, pulled on her dressing gown and went across the landing to her office. This was ridiculous and dangerous. What did she think she was playing at?

Maggie booted up her computer and began to compose an email.

Dear Max, thank you very much for lunch today, and for your time, and for showing me some of the things your slaves have to endure.

Her mind raced as the memories returned; was it endurance or enjoyment that lingered in her mind? Whichever it was she knew that however appealing the sensation it was also terrifying, perhaps too terrifying.

It was a real struggle to keep her mind on the task in hand, but even so she continued.

But I have, despite your parting words, come to the conclusion that I'm really not ready to be involved in the kind of activities you showed me – if I ever was. Thank you for your time.

Best, Maggie Howard.

She pressed *Send*, and as the message vanished into the ether she sat for a few moments wondering whether it was a great mistake or a narrow escape. Was it relief or a sense of loss that gripped her?

For a few minutes she stared out of the office window into the night sky, trying to still her racing mind by picking out the constellations she recognised. What devil was it that Max Jordan had released? Certainly without his influence she wouldn't have responded to Guido in the way she did. Maggie didn't see herself as a slave or as naturally submissive, but there was no denying the kick of excitement she had felt whilst being at the two men's mercy. Was it too late to put that particular genie back in the bottle?

She padded back to bed, and as she turned off the light and closed her eyes it was Max Jordan's face she saw.

Chapter Five

'So, how about coming out to dinner with me?' said Simon Faraday, leaning across his office desk.

Maggie, looking up from her computer screen, lifted an eyebrow quizzically. 'I'm sorry?'

She had popped in to work to sort out a few things for the piece she was writing on garden design and was – at least to the outside world – totally absorbed in what she was doing.

Simon's crooked smile didn't falter. 'I was just thinking, the last few times I've seen you, you've looked a bit down in the mouth. So I thought you could do with cheering up. There's this really nice little seafood restaurant on the coast and I just thought...'

Maggie put on a strained smile. She had assumed Max Jordan's response would be to try and persuade her to change her mind about his proposition, but what she hadn't been prepared for was the polite email accepting her decision and wishing her well. It was open now on her computer, and she'd read it over and over.

But that, of course, wasn't the end of it. In the week or so since their lunch date Maggie's dreams had been haunted by compelling images of Max Jordan and Guido, and in quiet moments during the day she found her mind recreating a stunning collage of erotic images from her encounter with them. Thinking about it made her wet and excited and left her longing for more. It was the sweetest torture. Maggie closed her eyes, trying to convince herself that if she starved this newfound hunger it would, eventually, wither and die.

'So, what do you think?' asked Simon.

Maggie looked up at him and blushed, hoping he couldn't see what had been in her mind and painfully aware that she hadn't listened to a word he'd said. 'I, um,' she began. 'The thing is, Simon, that I…'

'That I'll pick you up around eight, that's all settled then,' he said cheerfully.

'No, I?'

'We're going to the *Neptune*. It's so popular I was lucky to get a table at all.'

'Eight?' Maggie couldn't quite get her head around what was going on.

'Eight o'clock, that's right, tonight,' he insisted. 'What's the matter, not changed your mind already, have you?' he laughed.

She stared at him, bemused. Surely she hadn't agreed to go out with Simon Faraday whilst daydreaming about Max Jordan?

'I didn't say I'd go,' she said flatly; nothing was so important that she would have forgotten that.

He pulled a face. 'Oh come on, Maggie,' he pressed. 'You didn't say you wouldn't. And anyway, where's the harm? Everyone else is going to be there. This way you can have a drink, relax, and let me do the driving.'

Maggie shivered, recalling in graphic detail the last time someone had taken her for a drive.

'Eight it is, then,' he said, and before she could decline he was heading off across the office at top speed with a huge grin on his face. She looked back at the email and sighed. Maybe it wouldn't be such a bad thing; she could do with a night out. Maybe she was being cruel; maybe Simon Faraday wasn't so bad, really.

Perhaps he was an acquired taste. Perhaps he had hidden depths. Maggie sighed; who was she trying to kid?

'So who's going to the *Neptune* with the delectable Simple Simon from accounts then?' said one of the guys from of the graphics department on his way past her desk.

Maggie growled at him. Evidently bad news travels fast.

'What's all this about you and Simon Faraday, then?' said one of the other freelancers as she queued up in the deli at the end of the street at lunchtime.

By the time Maggie was ready to leave work she was seething. Was there nobody Simon hadn't told?

'Goodnight, Ms Howard, have a good one,' said the guy on the front desk as she crossed the reception area, and as she reached the glass doors he added, 'It's nice that you two have got together at long last. You'll make a lovely couple.'

There was no missing the sarcasm in the security guard's voice and Maggie swung round and glared at him, but he just grinned wryly.

So, it seemed that Simon had told every last soul that worked in the building, and Maggie was beside herself.

Supper was not a success.

'And then I hit it straight down the fairway, nearly three hundred yards, sweet as a nut,' Simon bragged, miming a golf swing.

Maggie looked at him over the rim of her wineglass. Over two hours with him and all she wanted to do was swing at the end of a rope. The 'everyone' Simon had said would be at the restaurant turned out to be a handful of minions and toadies from the accounting office. But at least one thing he was right about was the food, which was excellent, but by the time it was served she knew she had drunk too much to truly appreciate it. It had been a long and very dull evening.

She stifled a yawn, and when some little creep at the end of the bench said, 'Looks like someone's ready for bed,' half the table sniggered.

Simon caught her eye, and Maggie smiled in what she hoped was a neutral sort of way, at which he drained his glass and said, 'Well, it's getting late and we've all got a drive home. Think we should make a move.'

Maggie was about to protest, but then realised that she really did want to get home, and much more time spent with Simon and any pretext of good manners would have gone. So she got her coat and slipped outside.

'Someone's keen,' said the same creep as the rest followed her out into the car park.

As they reached Simon's car he opened her door, but then any sense of gallantry was lost as he grabbed hold of her arms.

Maggie wriggled out of his grasp but even so he pressed his lips to hers in some revolting parody of a passionate kiss. 'I've been wanting to do that all evening,' he rasped. 'God, you look bloody lovely. Good enough to eat.' There was no missing the implication in his tone, and Maggie glared at him.

They drove home in complete silence, Maggie only too aware of the wine in her bloodstream. Bloody man. She might have accepted his dinner date but that gave him no right to maul her, did it? Or was she giving him mixed signals? Did he, like Guido, think she was offering a ride for a ride?'

When they got back to her house it was obvious that Simon expected to be invited inside. Maggie glanced up at the windows; Kay couldn't be home yet, the lights were out in the sitting room and there were none on upstairs. Maybe she was staying over at Mike's.

'Simon,' she began. It was important to nip this in the bud before it went any further, but he smiled at her and slid his arm across the back of her seat.

Maggie sighed. 'Look, Simon, I'm really... really...' she decided upon the truth, 'I'm really pissed off that you told everyone at work that you were taking me out. That's not the way to do it...' He looked hurt and she felt a mixture of relief and contrition, but apparently undeterred he moved closer and this time she hadn't the heart to push him away. He took this as an invitation.

'Maggie, you've got no idea how long I've waited for this,' he whispered, pulling her close and kissing her full on the mouth, his tongue hungrily seeking entry between her lips. As he pressed closer one hand crawled onto her knee and before she could stop him it eased clumsily up her thigh while the other settled on her breast.

He began to move his lips against hers, and for the briefest of moments Maggie tried to let herself sink into it, go with the flow, respond in kind, imagining what it might be like to have Simon as a lover, but every instinct in her body fought against it. She didn't want it. She didn't want him.

Encouraged by her apparent passivity Simon's fingers tightened on her breast while the one between her legs tried desperately to find a way into her panties.

'Open you legs,' he murmured thickly. 'Come on, baby, you know you want me.'

'Simon, for God's sake,' she snapped, pressing against his chest. 'Of course I don't want you.'

'Relax,' he purred, still intent on seduction. 'Let me do the driving.'

Maggie was so stunned she didn't know what to say

until his fingertips grazed the lips of her sex and his panting increased in volume. 'Shit I've waited so long for this,' he drawled. 'You feel so good. Come on, open wider for me.'

'For crying out loud,' Maggie yelped, managing to wrestle free and scramble out of the car, 'stop it, Simon.'

Totally bemused he clambered out after her. 'What the hell's the matter?' he demanded. 'I thought it was going really well. Do you want to go inside instead, so we can get a bit more comfortable? I can understand you not wanting to make out in a car.' He looked at her intently, waiting for a reply, and then snapped angrily. 'What? I thought you liked me.'

Maggie shook her head. 'Simon, I need you to understand this,' she said slowly, as though talking to an imbecile – which perhaps he was, she thought. 'I don't fancy you. I've never fancied you, and I never will fancy you. No, I never will, not at all. You're not my type. I think of you as a friend.' She could hardly tell him he made her flesh crawl.

For a few moments Simon looked taken aback by her words, and then he smiled. 'Maggie, I understand what you're going through, and I don't want to rush you into anything you're not ready for. I really like and respect you, and we can take it as slowly as you want.'

Maggie stared at him in astonishment. If only he knew, she thought. She shook her head. 'No thanks, Simon,' she said. 'Goodnight and thank you for a lovely dinner.'

'What do you mean, goodnight?' he snapped angrily, as if the penny had finally dropped. 'Aren't you going to invite me in for a coffee or something?'

She shook her head again. 'No, it really isn't what I want, Simon,' she insisted. '*You* really aren't what I want. I'm trying not to be hurtful; I just want you to understand. I like working with you – but that's as far as it goes.'

'You little tease!' Simon snorted. 'You shouldn't lead men on like you do. You'll regret this, Maggie Howard. I promise you, you'll regret it.'

But she had already turned away feeling both sorry for Simon, and relieved to be away from him. She went up the path without looking back, closed the front door behind her and took a deep breath, waiting for the sound of his car pulling away.

After a minute or two standing in the dark of the hall she heard the roar of the engine and sighed with relief. There was something she had to do and she certainly wasn't going to do it with pining Simon lurking in the street outside.

She went upstairs, switched on her computer and began to type.

Dear Max...

She stared at the screen, trying to work out what it was she really wanted to say. She erased her introduction and began again.

You're right, there is no escape, she eventually continued. *Please may I...* She paused again. How did she ask, how did she let him know that she wanted more than anything else to feel again the kiss of his whip on her flesh? She opened the drawer of her desk and drew out the contract, and then with her heart in her mouth she began typing again.

Humbly beg to be trained by you?
Maggie.

She pressed Send before she had a chance to lose her nerve, and then sat in the darkness staring at the screen. Although she was nervous and worried about what she had just done, she also knew with total certainty that it was the right thing to do.

As the thought settled in her head she heard a noise – a hiss and then a sharp intake of breath. At first she thought it was her imagination, and then she realised with a start that she had made a terrible mistake. The house wasn't empty at all. Kay and Mike were in Kay's room and the noise Maggie had heard was the swat of the crop or a whip. Something in Maggie's belly tightened as she heard Kay's emotional voice call out the number of the stroke.

'One,' she squealed.

Maggie closed her eyes, her body and mind instantly alight with the memory of Max's touch. She crept across the landing and stood for a few seconds outside Kay's door. There was no way she wanted them to know she was there, spying on them, but part of her longed to join in. She heard the whistle of the crop again, and this time a guttural cry as the implement found its mark.

'Oh my, please master, please no,' Kay begged as the crop cracked down again.

Maggie shuddered, feeling her sex tightening, and tiptoed back to her room.

Lying alone in the darkness, all thoughts of Simon receding fast, she listened as Mike thrashed Kay. At twenty-five strokes it finally stopped, and Maggie closed her eyes, imagining the sensation as a hungry cock drove deep into her friend's cunt, filling her as her beaten buttocks ground back against his groin. It was almost more than she could bear. Without thinking she moved her hands down over her breasts, relishing their weight and softness in her palms, teasing the hardening peaks, and then when the need became greater still she moved on down across her flat tummy, finding herself wet and hot. Easing two fingers into the tight confines of her sex she began to circle the glowing bud of her clit, lifting her hips, imagining her fingers working in and out were a cock as she impaled herself again and again.

With her excitement being mirrored in the bedroom across the landing it didn't take long for her to bring herself to the point of no return. As she stroked and explored and let the waves of pleasure wash over her she imagined Max Jordan there in the darkness, watching her every move, his eyes glinting with desire.

Finally Maggie fell asleep with her fingers still between her thighs.

'I didn't hear you come in last night,' said Kay, helping herself to a cup of coffee, dressed in her bathrobe.

Maggie smiled and sipped her tea. 'I was late getting back,' she fibbed, wondering how Kay felt, imagining the pattern of marks on her silky smooth skin.

'And how did your romantic dinner go with the lovely Simon?'

Maggie laughed bitterly. 'It didn't. It was a bit of disaster, really. Did you go out anywhere nice?'

Kay shook her head. 'No, Mike came round and we had a nice quiet night in.'

'Right,' Maggie said casually. For a moment their eyes met, and strangely it was Maggie who blushed, not Kay.

'Are you working at home today?' said the latter, leaning easily against the kitchen unit.

'No,' said Maggie, glancing up at the clock. 'I'm working on some layouts for the garden features, and it's easier to do it at the office.'

Kay nodded. 'Okay, well in that case I'll see you later,' she said, and was gone, taking her coffee with her.

Maggie worked doggedly all morning, keeping her head down and ignoring all questions about the events of the night before from others in the office. Time and again her mind strayed to the sound of Kay crying out in the darkness, intermingled with images of Max and Guido and the way the crop had felt, the way her own body had writhed under its cruel kiss.

Fortunately Simon didn't show his face and by lunchtime she was feeling far less tense, except of course that she found herself checking the incoming email every ten minutes looking for Max's reply. As she stared at the screen countless thoughts ran through her head. What if he didn't respond? What if he didn't want her, after all? What if it had all been a huge mistake?

Before she drove herself mad with worry and self-doubt she decided to go down to the canteen and pick up a sandwich and coffee, and to her surprise when she got back there was a huge bunch of scarlet roses, broken by soft sprays of gypsophila, sitting on her desk. Her first reaction was to look around in case it was a joke. Or worse still, what if they were from Simon?

She put her coffee down on the desk and undid the little note attached to the swathe of cellophane.

Welcome home, slave. Check your email. Your master.

With her heart beating nineteen-to-the-dozen she logged on, and there, tucked amongst at least a dozen other messages was a single line email inviting her to pick up an e-card from a bondage site. As it opened she shivered with anticipation, for on the screen was an image that could have very easily been her. Tastefully shot in black and white a naked female knelt at the feet of a man in full evening dress, her hands bound behind her back with cord. She was wearing a collar, but most of all it was her face that struck Maggie. Her expression was serenely beautiful, totally at ease with her submission. Under the image Max Jordan invited her to begin her training.

I will pick you up at ten o'clock tomorrow morning, from your home. Make sure you bring the contract with you. Signed, unless you change your mind again. I shall expect you to stay overnight. You will wear a full-length coat, short dark skirt and white blouse, hold-up stockings and high heels. You will not wear any underwear, unless of course you wish to be punished.

Max Jordan had an unfailing eye for detail, thought Maggie. She smiled and looked back at the bunch of roses, remembering her punishment last time she got the instructions wrong. Oddly enough, it was a relief to know he wanted her and, stranger still, how much she longed to feel that sense of being owned.

'So what's this then, a little token of affection from a mystery admirer?' said a familiar voice.

Maggie looked up to find Simon standing alongside the desk. She quickly flicked off the screen so he couldn't see the picture on the card.

'Funny you should say that,' she said as casually as she could manage.

Simon managed a weak grin. 'About last night.'

'I think I owe you an apology, Simon,' she cut in, her resolve and confidence boosted by Max's invitation.

'I've been thinking, too,' he countered. 'Maybe I was taking things a bit too quickly. So to make it up to you I was wondering if you would like to come to the cinema with me at the weekend?'

Maggie smiled but shook her head. 'No thanks, Simon. I'm flattered, but I meant it when I said you really aren't my type.'

His expression soured immediately. 'So what is your type?' he sneered. 'Men who send you roses, I suppose.'

And with that he marched off across the office in a foul mood again.

Maggie sighed. Men who didn't behave like spoilt children would have been a better description. She looked back at the screen. Men like Max Jordan.

The following morning Maggie stood in her kitchen dressed exactly as she'd been instructed. She had one eye on the clock and shifted anxiously from foot to foot counting off the minutes. Waiting was awful. What if Max didn't show up? What if it was all a cruel joke? She gazed in the mirror – her eyes looked wild and haunted, and when the doorbell rang she almost jumped out of her skin.

It was a sunny, lovely day, oddly normal in contrast to the images and memories in her head. Guido was waiting for her on the doorstep, and if he had any thoughts about her appearance or their earlier encounter in the woods it didn't show on his face.

'Good morning, Maggie,' he said, and touched the peak of his driver's cap.

Maggie reddened, remembering their last encounter. 'Good morning.'

As she walked slowly away from the house she felt as if her life was about to change forever. As she got to the car Guido opened the nearside rear door, and to her surprise Max Jordan was waiting in the back.

He smiled and indicated that she should join him. 'Good morning, Maggie,' he said smoothly, as with her heart in her mouth she slipped in alongside him. 'How nice to see you again,' he said. 'And how are you today?' And then as the car drew smoothly away he added, 'So have you got the contract with you, as I instructed?'

Maggie nodded, not trusting herself to speak. She

opened her bag and handed him the envelope.

He nodded. 'Very good. Now, take off your clothes, except for your shoes and stockings.' His manner was firm and concise. Maggie stared at him questioningly, but his expression remained totally neutral. 'Already you disobey me?' he said. 'On one hand you beg to be allowed to serve and be trained by me, and then you fall at the first hurdle?'

Maggie looked around the interior of the car, anything rather than meet his eyes, shivering under his unflinching gaze. 'But... but I can't,' she ventured. 'Not here in your car.'

'Oh but you can, my dear, and you will,' he said confidently, 'because I have instructed you to do so and you will obey me. You want to. You need to surrender, Maggie. Now take off your clothes, I won't tell you again. Or would you rather we turned round and I took you home?'

'No,' Maggie blurted. 'The thing is...' her voice faded as she struggled with the reality of obedience.

Max appeared bored by her resistance and turned his attention to the envelope she'd given him. Ripping it open he pulled out the contract.

'So, Maggie,' he said, 'let us see what it is you've agreed to. "The slave will be under her master's complete and total control and will immediately obey and comply with any order or instruction given to her...' He smiled eruditely, before reading further. 'If the slave displeases or disobeys her master in any way she expects to endure any punishment he so chooses as necessary for her inappropriate actions...'

He studied her closely, his eyes bright. 'Well, my dear?'

Maggie dropped her gaze, and with a sigh of resignation, slowly unbuttoned her coat and slipped it back off her shoulders. As Max continued to read she unbuttoned and removed her blouse, unzipped her skirt and eased it down over her hips, until she was sitting beside him in just hold-up stockings and her high heels. She knew without looking up that Guido was watching her progress in the rear-view mirror.

'Very good, my dear,' Max said, as she folded her clothes on the seat. 'Here.' He handed her the collar she had worn so briefly at the hotel. Without a word she put it on and then turned slightly so he could snap the little lock shut. The sound made her shiver with anticipation.

Max looked her up and down appreciatively and then cupped one breast, rolling the nipple between thumb and forefinger. 'Open your legs.' His tone was crisp and businesslike.

Maggie stiffened. His fingers tightened on her nipple making her gasp, but still she resisted him. 'Maggie,' he growled, squeezing the bud between his fingertips, making her cry out in shock, and this time she let her knees fall apart.

With no prelude his free hand dropped into her lap, fingers roughly prising her sex open, exposing her totally. Maggie gasped; there was no finesse here, just a desire to explore her body in the basest of ways. He drove a finger between her lips, a sense of shame swamping her as he explored her delicate folds.

'Did you find her nice and tight, Guido?' he asked casually, and Maggie looked up in horror, reddening furiously. It hadn't occurred to her that Max would know about her escapades in the woods with his driver. She had assumed it was a secret between her and Guido – and knew in her heart that it would never have happened had it not been for the lingering image of slavery and submission Max Jordan had imprinted on her mind.

'Yes, sir,' said Guido, his eyes twinkling in the mirror. 'Nice and tight, and really hot for it.'

Max brushed her clitoris with his thumb, making the muscles in her belly tighten. Maggie could feel her body responding shamefully.

'So, you let Guido fuck you as soon as my back was turned, did you?' he accused her. 'Is that the kind of girl you are, Maggie? A dirty little slut who opens her legs to any man that comes along?'

What could she say? She felt sick with shame. There was no excuse for the way she'd behaved.

'From now on I will be in control of who has you – who fucks you.' He sank three fingers into her, making her stiffen and suppress a sob. 'And I will decide when you touch yourself and how you do it. You do touch yourself, don't you, Maggie?'

She closed her eyes and wished she could close her ears too, his words goading her.

'Tell me,' he ordered.

'Yes, master,' she admitted.

'Yes master, what?' he pressed. Surely Max didn't really want her to explain. A finger pressed hard over her clit, making her whimper beneath the heady mixture of discomfort and pleasure. 'Tell me, Maggie. Tell me.'

'I – I like to touch myself,' she stammered.

'Where do you like to touch, Maggie?' he interrogated. 'Your nice tits? Your cunt?'

Maggie felt the heat of humiliation growing inside her. How on earth could she say the words aloud? In the front of the car Guido listened and waited, his eyes on the road as he drove.

'Yes, master,' was all she could manage.

Max caught her clitoris tight between thumb and forefinger. 'Don't try and be clever with me, young lady. Tell me, do you like to touch this?' His hand spread to cradle her sex.

'Yes, master, I like to play with myself there,' she admitted meekly, her voice barely above a whisper.

Max nodded. 'Good girl.'

She felt defeated and crushed and humiliated. Max pulled her to him and kissed her forehead. 'Good girl,' he said again. 'Now, as you like the woods so much I thought we might go for a little walk today. Just you and me.' He handed her her coat. 'Put it on.'

Maggie looked at him inquisitively. Did he mean her to get dressed again? He smiled as if sensing her confusion, his voice as warm and personable as some older uncle taking his favourite niece out for the day. 'Just put it on as you are – no need to get dressed again.'

Gratefully she pulled it over her nakedness, but before she could button it he added, 'Leave it open, I want to look at you.' He carefully arranged the garment so that her body remained totally exposed to him, and then added to the bizarre quality of the journey by starting a conversation with her about her work at the magazine, and she found herself telling him about the project on gardens.

As time passed towns gave way to villages and villages gave way to countryside. Guido manoeuvred the car through the trees, along a track that led away from the winding road. The car drew to a halt in a small, leafy area that provided parking for picnickers and ramblers.

'Get out,' he ordered her, and Maggie was about to protest when he added, 'You may button your coat now, for the time being.'

She sighed with relief, for with her coat fastened and stockings on, no one would guess she was naked underneath; a little inappropriately dressed for a woodland stroll, perhaps, but certainly not naked.

Max caught hold of her hand. 'Now, my dear,' he said, 'let me show you one of my favourite places.'

They walked for a while through sun-drenched trees, talking about all manner of things, but just beneath the surface Maggie could feel her expectation and tension growing. There came a moment when silence fell and all she could hear was her pulse in her ears, a counterpoint to the gentle sounds of the woodland and nature.

Despite her coat she was very aware of her nakedness beneath, particularly every time a dog walker or courting couple ambled by, nodded and murmured politely and walked on.

At last Max headed off the main trail towards a thicket, stopped in a slight hollow and from behind a small bush produced several lengths of rope.

Maggie stared at him in astonishment. 'What are you going to...?' she began, her voice tight with apprehension.

'Take off your coat, Maggie,' was all he said.

As Max unwound the rope he watched her closely. It was interesting to watch her hesitation. She was torn between her desire, her fear, and a myriad other contradictory emotions. As if in slow motion she slipped her coat off, letting it fall to the ground. She stood very still in front of him, making no effort to cover herself, her nakedness emphasised beautifully by the trees.

As Max blindfolded her he could feel her trembling. He pressed the ball-gag into her mouth and then took hold of her wrists, feeling the tremor vibrate deliciously through her body. She looked magnificently vulnerable amongst their surroundings, her creamy skin a subtle contrast to the whispering canopy of green and gold.

She looked like a delicate nymph.

He bound her wrists tight together in front of her and then threw one end of the rope up and over a branch above her head, pulling it tight so that his newest student was stretched taut, taking her weight on the balls of her feet, hands bound high up above her head. With more rope he tied each ankle apart, spreading her legs wide.

She was totally still and silent, although as he worked he could feel every sense in her body reaching out to him, begging, hoping, searching for clues as to what might happen next. Standing behind her he ran his hands over her, both to enjoy her body and to reassure her. Her flesh was silky and cool.

She moaned behind the gag as his fingers worked down her spine and around her lithe torso to cup her breasts. She gasped, instinctively thrusting her body back towards him. Max smiled to himself; beneath her cultured and rather aloof exterior Maggie Howard had the heart of a whore. When he turned his attentions to her sex he discovered that she was already wet, her silky juices coating the tops of her thighs.

Stepping back he slipped off his jacket and took a flogger from the inside pocket. Very gently he drew the soft leather strands across her thighs and buttocks. Maggie mewled, tugging against the restraints. Max stepped back a little to check his stroke, and then hit her, not hard, but enough to make her muscles tense. She gasped and twisted at the end of the rope, instinctively trying to escape. He hit her again, harder, and she whimpered into the gag. Harder still he struck her and she let out a stifled sob, the noise spilling out from around the gag.

He beat her again and she shrieked as the tail of the cat wrapped around her ribcage and clawed hungrily at her breasts.

Max smiled. Through the trees he saw a flicker of movement and knew his activities were being observed. He hit her again, ignoring their uninvited guest, deliberately lower so that the tails of the flogger wrapped round the tender flesh of her thighs. Her whole body convulsed. Again she cried out, sharp and raw despite the gag, and then he struck again, from the corner of his eye spying an elderly man creeping closer, totally mesmerised by Maggie and her naked, whipped body.

Max hit her again and her head snapped back. He knew from the tone of her muffled protests that even though she was still at some level registering the pain, her mind was floating in a sea of endorphins, the body's natural pain relief.

The next blow wrapped around her waist and she twisted on the rope, gasping, saliva seeping around the gag onto her chin. Her body seemed to glow with an inner light as the pain speared through her. She looked superb, and Max glanced to his left and eyed the old man, his expression frozen with carnal hunger. It was as if Maggie's passion and pain had drawn him out into the open.

'Would you like a closer look?' asked Max.

The old man looked around uncertainly, clearly unable to believe his luck, and then nodded. It was obvious from the bulge in the front of his trousers that he was hugely aroused.

Maggie was trying hard to still her breathing as she reached out for clues as to what was happening. The old man circled her like a hungry scavenger, studying her beauty and her vulnerability, breathing it in. Max stepped close behind her and reached round to open the lips of her sex, so that the old man could see the ripe pinkness within. She was wet, her clit a hard bud longing for release. The old man leered and licked his lips, and fumbling with his trousers pulled out a gnarled and wizened cock.

Max beckoned him closer, so he could touch her, and feeling a second pair of hands on her flesh Maggie let out a shriek of dismay.

'Be nice to our new friend, my dear, or I'll take the whip to you again,' Max threatened, his lips brushing her ear.

The old man wiped his mouth and then ran his shaking hands over her face and throat, before cupping a breast in each hand, then moving even closer, lowered his lips hungrily over one nipple and sucked noisily. His twitching cock brushed against her thigh, leaving a sticky trail across her creamy flesh.

Maggie swallowed as if trying to still her fears, while the old man's fingers and lips pulled and slobbered on her breasts.

'Help me untie her,' said Max, and the old man needed no further encouragement. He stooped stiffly to untie her ankles, his face within inches of her sex, drinking in the enticing scent of her arousal.

Max untied her hands and then turned and eased her forward so that she was bent at the waist, her hands against the tree to support her. The old man leered again as Max undid his trousers and, without prelude, sank his raging cock into Maggie's waiting and vulnerable body.

She moaned and threw back her head, her sex closing around him like a clenched fist, her muscles drawing him deep, deep inside her. Despite the gag she cried out as Max began to fuck her. He could sense her longing for her own release, while beside them the old man groaned too and mauled her nearest breast while with his other hand he avidly pumped his straining shaft.

Max suspected that neither of them would last long. Maggie cried out as he pulled her back onto him again and again. The old man snorted and grunted and an instant later a flood of sperm hit her back and arm and then Max was there too, filling her with his offering.

As he pulled out of Maggie the old man sank slowly to his knees and began to lick hungrily at her quim and bottom. She mewled wearily and then Max watched as her body and her raw animal need began to take over. She began to move, instinctively grinding her wet quim over the man's wrinkled face until his tongue and fingers carried her over into oblivion, the waves of orgasm crashing over her. Between her trembling legs the old man, his face slick with sexual juices, pulled away, leering broadly. Max moved forward and rubbed his flaccid cock across her lips, and watched with satisfaction as her tongue emerged and she performed her duty for him. To his delight she drew his limp wet cock between her lips, and he enjoyed the devoted movements of her tongue.

Chapter Six

Back at the car Maggie sat quietly trying very hard to regain some sense of composure. She was wearing her coat, the leather slave collar, hold up stockings and shoes, the latter now a little grimy from their walk and activities in the woods. In the rear-view mirror Guido watched her discomfort with evident interest.

'Home now, I think,' Max decided, 'for a little lunch and relaxation. You can leave your clothes and bag in the car; Guido will see to them.'

Maggie had almost forgotten that she'd agreed to stay

with him, and realised with a growing sense of apprehension that whatever was going to happen to her, the experience in the woods was just the beginning.

Working from home meant that she could come and go as she pleased. Although she had a desk at the magazine's office no one would comment on her absence as long as her stories were filed on time. She sat back and closed her eyes, trying hard not to let her imagination run away with her. For a moment she tried to imagine what it might be like if she never went home. What if Max kept her? What if…? She bit her lip, struggling to get a grip on her rampant imagination.

Max Jordan's home was an elegant four-storey townhouse tucked away in an affluent city side street. They were welcomed at the door by his housekeeper, Mrs Griffin, a tall, sour-faced woman of an indefinable age. She was elegant and icy, dressed in a dove-grey coatdress that seemed deliberately cut to hide her figure, almost as if designed to render her asexual. Her thick straight hair, a shade of grey fractionally lighter than her dress, was pulled back into a severe bun that did nothing at all to soften her angular features or cold blue eyes.

'Would you like me to take your coat?' she said to Maggie as they made their way inside. Maggie stopped mid-stride, and Max turned to look at her. It was obvious that he expected her to hand it over, and Maggie was beginning to understand only too well that it didn't do to keep Max Jordan waiting or to disobey him. The rules of the game weren't so hard to fathom out, but were at odds with everything else she had ever believed in or known. She slipped off the coat and handed it to Mrs Griffin, painfully aware of her exposure, but the older woman's expression didn't change, she said nothing, her eyes taking in both

Maggie's nakedness and her discomfort in a single glance.

'Give Mrs Griffin your shoes as well, Maggie, they need cleaning,' Max said, and naked, barefoot, feeling like a well-trained puppy, Maggie padded along behind him into an elegant sitting room furnished with black leather chesterfields and a cream carpet. The drapes at the floor to ceiling windows were black velvet caught back with gold ties, and the room had an air of male elegance, of good taste and understated luxury.

'Today, my dear, you will begin basic training, you will begin to understand how it feels to be a fulltime slave. This evening we have guests coming for supper. But now we will have a little aperitif, lunch, and then I'll have Mrs Griffin show you to your room. You might like to have a little rest before this evening.'

He smiled and settled comfortably on one of the sofas. 'I would suggest you take a nap. It will be a long evening. Now turn around; I want to see if you're marked.'

Maggie did as she was told, reddening slightly as Max turned her first one way and then the other. 'Hardly anything,' he said, sounding disappointed. 'I like to see where I've been, to leave my mark. Go to the side table and bring me my crop.'

Maggie hesitated.

'Did you hear me?' he asked.

'Yes, master,' she said. 'I heard you.'

'Then do as you're told. For a little while you will be allowed some leeway, but trust me, young lady, that luxury will rapidly be coming to an end.'

Maggie went over to the table, where set out in a neat row was a braided leather crop, a whip, the tails arranged in straight lines, a schoolmaster's cane and a leather paddle that looked a little like a short oar.

The tools of Max's trade.

Maggie gulped and picked up the crop as instructed, then with her eyes downcast she returned and handed it to him.

'Get down on your hands and knees,' he ordered.

Maggie got to the floor in front of him, already feeling the rush of adrenaline, stunned at how quickly she obeyed. She remembered how the crop bit into her flesh and made her cry out in shock and pain. Closing her eyes she braced herself for what she knew would follow.

Max, the consummate sadist, trailed the looped tip gently along her spine and over her buttocks, exploring her body with all the self-assurance of a man examining his property.

'Open your legs,' he said, and Maggie obeyed, exposing the delicate folds of her sex. Max cut the air with the crop, a practice swing, but still it made the kneeling girl cringe. 'You're a little nervous, slave,' he commented.

She heard the crop cutting the air again and cried out almost before the blow cracked down across her poor bottom. Even though it wasn't overly hard it sent a white-hot glow through her body.

'One,' she hissed instinctively, knowing it was what he wanted to hear.

'Two,' she wailed as the next strike landed square across the fullest part of her buttocks.

'*Three...*' The pain was intensifying.

'Four,' she gasped. It hurt so much, hot and sharp.

'Five.' The word nearly caught in her throat, vying with a protest for release.

'Six.' Surely Max would stop soon? Surely six was enough?

'Seven... eight... nine... ten...' a volley of rapid

strokes.

'Eleven... twelve!' Maggie shrieked, biting her lip to hold back the tears that threatened. And then it was over and she felt Max's cool hands on her skin, comforting the reddening flesh.

'There we are, my little one, all done,' he murmured, and for an instant Maggie sensed and heard the arousal in his voice. He pressed the crop to her lips and without a moment's hesitation she kissed it. How had this happened?

Gently Max helped her to her feet. 'Look,' he said, and stood her in front of a large mirror. Maggie turned and looked at her bottom, the blotchy welts rising across both cheeks. Max slipped a hand between her thighs and she closed he eyes with a mixture of shame and resignation, knowing without being told that her rogue body was wet already and eager for more.

'Now, get me a sherry and then come and kneel at my feet like a good slave,' he said, and Maggie did as she was told, aware of his eyes on her as she moved around the room. Then she handed him his drink and knelt at his feet on the carpet, and he idly stroked her hair as he talked.

'Our guests tonight know you have only just begun your training, but that is no reason for bad behaviour,' he said. 'You will do exactly as you are told, when you are told. Do you understand me?'

'Yes, master,' she acknowledged.

Max smiled. 'I understand this is hard for you, my dear, but you must trust me. I will show you things that until now you have only dreamed of.'

Although he was speaking quietly the tone was strong, the tone of man who had experienced many things, who commanded respect, and without thinking she settled her cheek on his knees, relishing the feel of his fingers stroking her head. It struck her as odd that a man who could be so cruel was also so capable of such tenderness.

Max sat for a while, soothing her as he might a favourite pet, and as he did she felt the tension in her easing. How odd that this man who gave her so much pain was also the one to offer her such a compelling sense of comfort and reassurance.

'So, as I said, we'll have lunch and then you can rest, my little one,' he said, then sipped his sherry.

'Yes, master,' she whispered, and realised how natural the words were beginning to sound.

Maggie's room was on the top floor, tucked up under the eves of the large old house, with a small en suite bathroom attached. The antique pine bed was made up in delicate white bed linen, and fluffy white towels hung from a rail by the open bathroom door. On one wall hung a large ornate mirror, and on a linen chest under the window a vase of white jasmine filled the room with a heady scent.

While she and Max had been downstairs having lunch her clothes were being neatly hung in the wardrobe, her clean shoes neatly tucked onto the bottom rail.

Then once Mrs Griffin had drawn the curtains and turned down the duvet, Maggie slipped into bed and despite everything going on in her life was asleep in a matter of seconds.

For a few moments when she awoke Maggie wondered where on earth she was. The light had subtlety changed as the day slipped slowly from afternoon into evening, and refreshed by her sleep she sat up in bed wondering what she was expected to wear for the dinner party. She'd brought a couple of nice outfits with her that could be dressed up or down as the occasion required. Maybe she ought to try and find her way downstairs and ask Mrs Griffin.

Just as she was considering what to do there was a knock on the bedroom door and the housekeeper appeared, and she quickly pulled the bedclothes up to cover her nakedness.

'The master sent me up to help you get ready,' the woman announced, her expression unchanged.

'I'm fine, thanks, really,' said Maggie pleasantly. 'There's really no need to go to any trouble. I was wondering what I ought to wear though?'

'The master sent me up to help you, Miss Howard.' The woman smiled thinly. 'Surely you know better than to disobey his instructions. I'm to bathe you, wash your hair and then help you dress.' As she spoke she set a box down alongside the vase of jasmine.

'Oh,' Maggie said, a little surprised by the announcement, not sure that she wanted to be treated like a child by the woman. 'And what am I to wear for this evening?'

Mrs Griffin's expression still didn't alter. 'You'll find out in good time.'

Maggie got up, and conscious of her nakedness she headed into the bathroom to use the toilet, when it struck her there was no door.

She looked back at Mrs Griffin, blushing furiously, but if she was expecting sympathy or privacy, none was forthcoming.

'I need to use the loo,' she said, but the woman seemed oblivious to her sensitivities. She followed her into the en suite, bent to put the plug in the bath and turned on the taps, but made no attempt to avert her gaze or leave Maggie alone. Defeated, Maggie sat on the toilet, careful not to catch the other woman's eyes.

When she was done Mrs Griffin added a stream of bath oil that filled the room with the scent of sandalwood and ylang ylang, and helped her step into the deep tub.

Maggie hadn't been bathed by anyone since she was a child, but Mrs Griffin lathered and then rubbed her down, her fingers skilfully working through her hair, down over her breasts and belly, and lower still into the intimate places between her legs. Maggie, although deeply embarrassed, knew it was pointless to resist. It was an odd thing to share so intimate an experience with a complete stranger, and sensual on the most basic of levels. She wondered if the woman could sense the flutter of arousal and pleasure in her belly, but if she did it was not apparent.

When she was done Mrs Griffin held out a fluffy white bath towel and dried Maggie with brisk efficiency.

'Stand still,' Mrs Griffin instructed, standing her in front of the large mirror while she oiled Maggie's body. Maggie shivered, but Mrs Griffin's face remained unerringly impassive while her skilled hands carried on rubbing her breasts, nimble fingers working over her nipples, tweaking them into hardness, sliding down over her tummy, sex, and the ripe curves of her bruised bottom. Maggie blushed furiously, but it seemed to go unnoticed as the woman worked diligently.

Behind the two-way mirror in the small room, little bigger than a cupboard, Max enjoyed a deep mouthful of brandy and settled down to watch Maggie being dressed, enjoying the familiar stirring in his groin.

When she was done the older woman opened the box on the linen chest, and as she lifted out the contents Maggie gasped in shock. Inside was a black leather harness, held together with rings and studs. It went around her torso like a jacket, large rings fitting tight over her breasts, forcing the nipples to jut forward. Straps snapped onto the D-rings on her collar, with another broad strap fastening tightly around her waist, and then between her legs was another one, with a slit in it so that once securely fastened in place it held the lips of her sex open. She swallowed hard and looked across at the housekeeper.

'It doesn't pay to keep the master waiting,' said Mrs Griffin.

Once Maggie was dressed the austere housekeeper handed her a pair of high-heeled knee-length boots, and then looked her up and down before very carefully outlining her eyes in dark brown kohl and her lips in red lipstick. Caught in the reflection of the dressing table mirror Maggie looked like a sexual toy, ready and available, her body a sexual invitation.

Mrs Griffin took a step back to admire her handiwork, and then as a final touch took a lead out of the box and snapped it to one of the D-rings.

Maggie felt a chill; it defined her status. Then she obediently rose and followed Mrs Griffin downstairs, her stomach churning.

'Ah, there you are, Mrs Griffin,' said Max, looking up as they entered the room. 'I was just telling Freya that you've cooked venison for us this evening.'

'Yes, Mr Jordan, although it's farmed,' said the housekeeper, entering into a conversation about cooking with Max's guest, a statuesque blonde dressed in a smart pinstriped business suit. She was sipping a cocktail and didn't even bother to look in Maggie's direction. But what really caught Maggie's attention was the naked man crouched on all fours at the woman's feet. He too was wearing a harness and a collar and lead. He looked at Maggie, drank her in, his eyes bright with lust and a very obvious hunger.

Max noticed Maggie looking at the man, and Freya caught the man looking at Maggie and admonished him sharply. 'Beau!' she said, snapping the lead taut and wrenching his neck.

'Sorry, mistress,' he whined, and Max smiled as Maggie's face registered her surprise and discomfort.

'On your knees, Maggie,' he commanded, and she knelt at his feet, trying to avoid the longing look of Freya's slave. She noticed that around his cock and balls, which were shaved and oiled, was a series of rings and leather straps, linked to the harness that appeared to keep him in a state of semi-arousal.

Mrs Griffin departed to the kitchen and Freya and Max were talking again. Under normal circumstances, at any normal dinner party, Maggie would have been chatting with them, or at least been politely involved in their conversation, a glass of quality wine in her hand. But here, crouched on the floor, it seemed that their chatting bore no relation to her life or where she was in the order of things.

Guido, smartly dressed in the guise of a butler, appeared and announced that dinner was served. Max smiled to his beautiful guest. 'Ah, splendid,' he said. 'Shall we, dear Freya?' and indicated that she should accompany him.

Freya again tugged Beau's leash and to Maggie's total amazement the man scurried behind her on all fours. When Max took her lead she looked up at him in silent appeal.

'Come on, Maggie,' he said, and to her shame she also followed on her hands and knees behind him, cringing with the degradation of it all.

'Nice markings,' Freya said casually, her fingertips brushing Maggie's welted buttocks. Max nodded his appreciation for the compliment; in that instant Maggie felt more like a prize possession than ever.

Across the hallway heavy double doors led into an elegant dining room, decorated in cream and the richest crimson.

A long mahogany table, set with crystal and silver and an ornate silver candelabrum, dominated it. Without being told Beau got to his feet and pulled Freya's chair out. Maggie decided she'd better follow suit for her master, and noticed the magnificent table was laid for only two.

Only two place settings?

She was hungry and had assumed, wrongly and somewhat foolishly it now seemed, that they would all be dining together. Instead Guido handed her a dish and indicated that she should serve Freya and Max, and as she began to she noticed that on a sideboard were two heavy-bottomed dog bowls. As she completed and task and set the serving dish down Guido nodded towards the bowls. She looked at him uncertainly, and then realised that she was supposed put food into them too – food she knew was for Beau and for her. She stiffened and stood her ground, but Guido nodded again and reluctantly she spooned vegetables into the two bowls, and then Beau added meat.

She looked down at the food. No knives, no forks, just fingers and tongues – like animals. This was impossible, but then Guido nodded towards the table where Beau was shaking out a linen napkin and settling it on Freya's lap. The elegant blonde appeared to take no notice of her slave; instead she gave Max her full attention, laughing gaily at some comment he'd made. Maggie looked at Max, who gave her an almost imperceptible nod of encouragement, so she shook out his napkin and dropped it onto his lap. He rewarded her by running a hand over her thigh, but it did very little to settle her.

Beau served the wine, while Max and Freya continued chatting. Beau then stood beside his mistress until she looked up and said, sounding decidedly bored with his presence, 'You may go and eat now.'

Guido placed both bowls on the floor side by side. Beau was immediately on his hands and knees again to eat, while Maggie stood looking down at him and the vacant dish. Guido had cut the food up into small pieces, and she was very hungry, but there was no way she was going to grovel like Beau.

'Is there something wrong with your dinner?' said Max, and it was obvious from his tone that he didn't take kindly to having his meal interrupted.

'No, master,' Maggie said contritely.

'Then eat it,' he ordered, and indicated the bowl with a sharp hand gesture.

Maggie looked at him beseechingly. 'Please, master, I can't,' she began, her voice quavering. There was no way she was going to eat like an animal, no matter how hungry she was. Meanwhile Beau was snaffling up his dinner like some obscene parody of an obedient pet dog.

'Can't, or won't?' said Freya icily.

Maggie looked down at her feet, painfully aware of her nakedness, accentuated rather than covered by the leather harness.

'Answer me!' the blonde snapped angrily, her veneer of refined elegance vanishing in an instant.

There was a long pause while Maggie summoned her resolve, and then at last she said determinedly, 'Won't.' She was instantly aware of the tense silence in the room as Max, his guest, and Guido all stared at her in apparent disbelief, and the grovelling man beside her stopped shovelling his face into the bowlful of food and looked up at her, his chin and nose smeared in rich sauce and his mouth open in shock.

'Won't, *mistress*,' Beau whispered sarcastically, but it was too late for Maggie to retract her insolence.

'Take her away!' Max roared at Guido, waving his hand in dismissal and throwing his linen napkin onto the table beside his meal, as though she had just ruined his appetite and the whole evening. 'Get her out of my sight!'

'Big mistake,' said Guido, as he marched Maggie out of the dining room and down the hall. 'Showing him up in front of his guests. Big mistake.'

'But I didn't,' Maggie protested.

Guido snorted. 'That's not how he'll see it.' He led her upstairs, unlocked a door at the far end of the landing, and pushed her inside, the room beyond making Maggie gasp with shock.

It was a dungeon. There was no other word for it. In one corner was an awful rack, and in another a large, foreboding cross-shaped frame. The walls were hung with whips and crops and gags and manacles, clamps and clips and all manner of other things, many of which Maggie didn't recognise and had no idea what they might be used for.

She turned to Guido. 'Let me go back,' she pleaded, unnerved by the ominous room. 'I'll eat my dinner, I will, it was a mistake. Just take me back. Honestly Guido, it was a silly mistake.'

Guido's smile widened. 'You're right about that,' he said, 'but it's too late to go back now. I suggest you cooperate, because if you don't it will be worse for you... a lot worse.'

Maggie shivered. What choice was there for her?

'Come closer,' he ordered, and caught hold of her

wrists.

A while later, after he and Freya had eaten and taken coffee and brandy, Max opened the door of the dungeon room and smiled. Guido had done a good job on his little charge. Maggie was nicely bound, blindfolded, her neck and arms held in a padded wooden yoke, holding her reasonably comfortably with her arms at shoulder level, her legs spread wide apart and manacled to a metal spreader-bar.

He watched his latest acquisition straining to turn, trying to make out who was there and what would follow. Beside him Freya smiled appreciatively and unfastened her tailored jacket, beneath which she wore a shiny black leather bodice. As he watched she dropped the jacket and then her skirt, rather like a seductive snake shedding its skin. Beau appeared and hurriedly picked them up, folding them neatly over a chair, his eyes bright with anticipation as his mistress stripped down to her beautifully styled leather basque. It was cut high to make the most of her long legs and the creamy flesh of her shapely thighs.

'May I?' she asked Max, without taking her eyes off Maggie's restrained form.

He smiled. 'Of course, my dear,' he said. 'Help yourself.'

Maggie trembled, responding anxiously to his voice.

Freya smiled calculatingly and surveyed the tools on offer, before taking down a fine leather whip.

In the restraints Maggie stiffened as she felt the approach of what for her was an unseen figure.

Freya walked around her, surveying her with assurance, pinching her nipples, feeling between her legs, pushing a finger deep inside Maggie's vulnerable sex and then drawing the slick juices out and across

Beau's waiting lips. He licked her fingers and whined expectantly for more.

'Nice and tight, Max,' the woman purred appreciatively. 'What's her arse like?'

Max smiled. 'Untried, Freya,' he disclosed. 'It's early days yet and you know my policy; it is for me and me alone. At least the first time.'

Freya laughed, the cultured sound like a tinkling piano. 'You are such a traditionalist, dear Max,' she mused. 'And besides, she'd need stretching whoever fucks her tight little virgin rear passage. Perhaps I can help you with that?' She ran her fingers over Maggie's buttocks, before working them into the warm valley between them.

Max watched Maggie react to the blonde's conversation with interested, seeing the tension in her neck and back, catching the slight nibble of her lower lip.

Beau whined again and leant up against Maggie's legs, like a cat, his expression hungry, and Freya's expression betrayed her affection and indulgent attitude towards her slave. She nodded and he began to touch and stroke, his fingers and tongue working into Maggie's wet quim.

The bound girl shivered as Freya drew the soft strands of the whip across her hips. They dangled against Beau's face and shoulders but he seemed oblivious to them, far keener to explore Maggie's undefended sex.

'Enough,' Freya snapped, and barely pausing for Beau to crawl clear she brought the whip down across Maggie's back. The strands wrapped around her, catching her breasts and making her jerk and shriek, although Max guessed that in her heighten state of anticipation even the lightest blow would extract such a reaction.

'One!' she gasped, her muscles tightening.

Freya laughed. 'Oh, there is no need to count tonight, my dear,' she said. 'There will be too many to keep track of.'

After six strokes Max held up a hand and took something else down from the wall. Freya's eyes sparkled approvingly. 'What a wonderful idea, dear Max,' she purred. 'How very remiss of me.'

Behind her mask Maggie was struggling with a sense of panic, and worse still, the warm glow of pleasure that was already gathering in her belly. What dark magic was this? She closed her eyes tight shut. It was as if Max Jordan had opened a doorway in her soul into a world she had never really believed existed.

A female hand cupped her breast, and she smelt expensive perfume. Freya pinched her nipple between finger and thumb and then drew it between her lips and sucked. She groaned against the supple flesh and began to tease Maggie's sex, teasing the wet lips that were held open by the split leather harness. Maggie wriggled, trying to get away from the fingers, although she knew she was already treacherously wet.

'Oh, don't struggle, honey,' purred Freya, her tone heavy with sensual intent, and an instant later something snapped onto Maggie's right nipple, making her cry out in shock and pain, and immediately the hurt was repeated on her other nipple. Maggie writhed desperately, trying to get away from the intense pain of the clamps as they chewed her erect buds.

'Gently, my pretty,' murmured Freya, and Maggie shivered, letting the sensation settle. It was hot and raw and made her eyes fill with tears, but after a few moments by some miracle her body began to adjust, as if, once the pressure was understood, it could cope. She took a long low breath, letting her body and mind settle. It was going to be all right after all, wasn't it?

And then Freya pinched the lips of her sex. Maggie froze, felt the brush of some kind of clamp on the delicate folds of flesh, and held her breath. 'Please, no... no,' she gasped. 'No...'

The jaws sprang shut and Maggie screamed. The pain was like nothing she had ever felt and tears meandered down her cheeks.

'Steady,' consoled Freya, pressing her lips to Maggie's. 'Don't fight it, breath slowly and relax into it. It will be all right, just breath slowly.'

Maggie tried to accept the throbbing discomfort, and then felt Beau licking her again.

'That's enough now, slave,' Freya intervened, and this time Maggie moaned not with pain but with frustration as the grovelling tongue left her.

Then before she had time to compose herself she heard something cut through the air and then screamed again as the cane found its mark. Her body thrust forward and Freya caned her again across her defenceless bottom. The first scream seemed to have barely died before another surpassed it. As her body arched the clamps on her nipples and labia seemed to bite even harder.

Maggie thought she would go mad from the torment, and then there was another stroke as brutal as the first two. Her nipples ached and her buttocks glowed. Again the blows exploded, and again and again. Maggie could hear someone sobbing and begging for mercy, and realised it was her.

Max's fingers tightened around his brandy glass. His cock ached with desire as Maggie sobbed and writhed deliciously in her restraints. She was truly magnificent. Her toned body was covered with a gloss of perspiration, her whole being alight with the pain, and yet he could also sense the tide of arousal behind it. Beau crouched at her feet like a dog waiting for leftovers. Freya's eyes were like glowing coals, her mouth open, her expression alive with excitement and anticipation.

At last she dropped the cane on the floor and grabbed Maggie's hair, wet with sweat and oil. 'Had enough?' she spat breathlessly.

'Yes, mistress,' Maggie sobbed.

'Good.' Freya caught hold of the clamps on her nipples and pulled her closer still. 'You will do as you're told next time.'

Maggie gasped with pain. 'Yes, mistress,' she promised. 'I will, mistress.'

Freya pulled off the clamps and Maggie wailed again as the woman massaged the blood-flow back, the apparent kindness a double-edged sword for the rush of blood was all the more painful for the stimulation. The clamp on Maggie's sex lips was also removed and then Freya looked at Guido, who was watching with interest.

'Get her out of the stocks,' she ordered, and as Maggie slumped to the floor the woman unfastened the crotch of her leather basque.

Max watched keenly. He suspected that Maggie had never been with another female before, and wondered how she'd react. If she refused to comply with Freya's demands, he knew the severe blonde would have no hesitation in meting out yet more punishment. With Maggie on her knees Freya cupped her face and pulled her to her sex. Freya really was a natural dominatrix, her pleasure truly in inflicting pain and exacting total obedience from those few who passed her stringent selection tests. Max knew she would be ready now for that growing pleasure to be brought to its natural conclusion. He smiled; on many occasions it had been him who'd had the pleasure of taking her to the very edge and beyond.

Crouched on the floor Maggie shivered. There was an instant, a split second when she pulled back with misgivings and revulsion, and then slowly she pressed a kiss to Freya's shaven mound, her tongue inquisitively slipping between the outer labia, easing them apart.

Freya sighed and beckoned to Guido to bring her one of the low dungeon stools. Then sitting upon it she opened her legs wide. 'Use you fingers as well as you tongue,' she instructed, and without hesitation Maggie complied, any resistance quashed. Beau crawled over and unfastened the leather laces of Freya's basque, exposing shapely breasts, and then sucked one nipple deep into his mouth. Guido looked to Max, who nodded, and the driver sank to his knees to suck the other, his erect cock in his hand.

It was all far too much to resist, so Max also got to his knees, but behind his slave girl and pressed a hand between her legs. She moved against him instinctively and he could smell her arousal. He unfastened his trousers and with one long penetration he drove his cock deep into Maggie's sex, and was rewarded by a guttural moan of pleasure as he filled her completely.

Maggie felt the first traitorous ripples of an orgasm reverberate through her body, and knew they weren't hers alone. Above her Freya moaned in delight, and she could hear the guttural snorts of the men as they approached their own orgasms. The climax, when it came, was rapid and destructive, like a hurricane ripping through her, tearing her and the others apart.

She heard Freya cry out and felt her grip her head and pull her face even tighter to her sex, anointing Maggie's mouth with her slick pleasure. She felt a splash on her shoulder, and another on her opposite arm and her back, and felt as if she was drowning in the men's spunk, while deep inside her she felt the final throbbing surge that told her the man thrusting between her legs had filled her with his seed.

Chapter Seven

Maggie woke in the half-light, wondering where on earth she was. A hand was between her thighs, lazily exploring the contours of her sex, stirring her from a dreamless sleep. As she tried to turn over she realised with a start that her hands were secured to a long chain that bound her to a bed. It was Max Jordan's bed. Images and events of the previous evening flooded her slowly awakening brain, and not just images, but also Max's instructions, his rules and constraints, which she must learn to obey as second nature. Max Jordan's rules.

'Slaves are not allowed to urinate in private, nor bathe without their master's permission.'

They had been drinking brandy after Freya and Beau had left in the small hours of the morning, and Max told her exactly what she must expect and adhere to if she continued in his service.

'You will be beaten every time we meet,' he told her. 'Ideally you should be beaten every day, but for the time being we must content ourselves with every meeting. Before your punishment you will tell me the things you have done that you think might displease me.' As he spoke he watched her expression intently, although she wasn't sure whether it was to watch for any sign of dissension or just because he enjoyed observing her reactions.

'From now on,' he continued, 'I will decide who uses your body, and that includes masturbation. These are just a few of the fundamentals, Maggie. When you signed the contract you became mine – body and soul. You fully understand that, don't you?'

Maggie nodded, tired and sated, the brandy relaxing her, unable to believe that a man of his age still had the stamina to go on when all she wanted was to fall into bed and sleep.

Max savoured a mouthful of the amber liquid, and then continued. 'When you are here and sleeping in my bed you are to wake me in the morning by sucking my cock.

'Your body is always to be available to me, or any person I choose.

'Whenever you are awaiting my presence, or any of my guests, unless told otherwise you will always assume the slave position – on all fours, legs apart, head down. Do you understand me, Maggie?'

She nodded sleepily. It was all too much to take in. Her whole body ached, her mind ached and she wanted to sleep, but Max continued. 'And from now on, until otherwise instructed you will keep every weekend free for my pleasure. Guido will pick you up every Friday evening. Other than toiletries you will only need to bring the clothes you stand up in. And whilst on the subject of clothes, as a slave you are forbidden to wear underwear unless it is something I have given you to wear for a specific purpose. This includes when you are at home, out shopping, or at work.'

'But what if someone notices?' said Maggie, instantly thinking of Simon Faraday at work.

Max smiled. 'Such trivialities are unimportant,' he said, easily dismissing her concerns.

'But what if they say something, or use the knowledge to try to take advantage of me?' she asked anxiously.

'Then you are to let them,' he said simply. 'After all, you are a slave now, Maggie. Indulge any such liberties, and then you must report to me every last detail.'

She blushed.

'So,' he said, draining the last of his glass. 'It is time for bed now, my little one. Oh, and one more thing, if I want you at any other time I will ring and have Guido collect you.' He produced a mobile phone and passed it to her. 'This is for you, to be used exclusively for communication between us.'

Maggie took it and nodded.

Totally exhausted, she had assumed that once they were upstairs she would be allowed to sleep, but instead Max had her kneel at the side of the bed and then used her mouth, fucked her as hard there as he had her cunt, then holding her close he filled her mouth with his seed and she had little choice but to swallow every last drop.

Before she had joined him in bed he put leather cuffs on her wrists and fastened her by a silver chain to the head of the bed. As the lock snapped shut he smiled. 'Sweet dreams, slave,' he said, and switched off the light.

Now, in the half-light of the bedroom and wide-awake, Maggie remembered her instructions, eased down under the bedclothes, took his flaccid penis between her lips and very gently began to suck. Her reward was a low chuckle of approval.

'Good girl, good girl,' he mumbled. 'But I want a little something more than your mouth this morning.' He pulled her up to him and stroked her hair back off her brow. 'Come with me,' he said, reaching over to get the key from the bedside cabinet drawer to unlock her wrists.

Max led her across the bedroom to his en suite bathroom, and turned on the shower. He then slipped off his robe and pushed her down to the floor. 'Hands and knees,' he snapped, and Maggie stared up at him in surprise. 'Now,' he insisted impatiently, taking a tube of lubricant from the glass shelf over the basin.

She obeyed, and before she had time to absorb what was happening she felt him work some grease into her anus and immediately felt him crouch behind her and press his erection between her buttocks. She held still, too apprehensive to resist, and felt his cock relentlessly sinking into her tight channel, deeper than she thought possible. Slowly her body gave way to him, filling her until she could feel his balls nestling against the lips of her empty sex. She whimpered, the experience so at odds with everything she had ever considered acceptable.

Max grunted with pleasure. 'Oh yes...' he growled under his breath as he began to move. 'Does it hurt?'

'A little,' she whispered truthfully. 'But it's not the pain. It's just...' How could she explain that it made her feel humiliated? He must surely know what he was doing to her, that in some ways what she felt was worse than any physical discomfort, and yet at the same time strangely, wickedly exciting? Crouched on the floor in the bathroom Max Jordan had reduced her to the lowest common denominator. Kneeling and naked for his pleasure she was only a sexual object, a pleasure to be taken, a good tight fuck. Tears ran down her cheeks as he ploughed deep into her rectum, her cries seeming to drive him on to greater effort.

She was terrified he might hurt her, terrified he might stop and terrified of the strange excitement building low in her belly. What was happening to her?

Above her Max's breath was becoming ragged, his

thrusts more instinctive, and Maggie found herself moving with him, longing to slide a hand between her legs to stroke her treacherous, throbbing clit.

'Please, master, may I touch myself?' she whispered, her breath heavy with trepidation and desire.

'Oh yes, my little one, you certainly may,' he snorted as he gripped her hips and pulled her back onto him. So Maggie began to rub her clit, feeling the little bud pulsing under her fingertips, but before she could orgasm Max ejaculated, driving furiously deep, and denied her own release Maggie slumped to the floor tiles, stunned and trembling, his penis pulsing rhythmically inside her tightness. Then when completely drained of his essence Max withdrew and gathered her limp form into his arms.

'Well done, slave,' he said, kissing her ear.

Maggie pressed herself into his embrace, seeking warmth and reassurance, and oddly enough, comfort. Gently he helped her to her feet and together they stepped into the shower. His hands worked over her body, lathering her, his washing her both an act of tenderness and an act of possession. She leant against him, giving him free rein to touch and explore her. His fingers pressed back and forth over her pleasure bud, and then he pulled down the showerhead and played it between her legs. Maggie gasped as the fierce jets found their mark. Skilfully he teased it back and forth over her clitoris and the succulent flesh of her sex and bottom, and she immediately felt the first glowing ripples of an orgasm wash over her.

'Ooohhhh…' she gasped.

'Don't forget to ask,' he warned, nipping her neck and shoulders.

'Please, master, please let me come,' she obediently begged. '*Please.*'

'Very well, you may,' he acquiesced, and gratefully she began to move against the powerful water jets, pressing her hips forward until she thought she could take no more, at which point Max sunk to his knees and gently began sucking her engorged clit. She cried out, this time in pure bliss, and let the sensations absorb her. She held him, crying out in delight, aware only of her body and the relentless ministrations of his tongue. Under his skilful manipulations the wonderful orgasm seemed to go on and on until she thought she would faint from the sheer intensity of feelings and emotions.

At last, after what seemed like an eternity, there was stillness with only the sound of the cascading water. Trembling, Maggie didn't resist as Max helped her out of the shower and wrapped her in a fluffy white towel.

'I have to get on with my day now,' he told her, slipping on his towelling bathrobe. 'I have things to attend to. I want you to go back to bed and rest; it's still early and there's no need for you to be up yet. I'll have Mrs Griffin bring you up some tea and sort out your clothes for the day.' He kissed her forehead and she padded back to the bedroom, and with a sense of relief, slipped between the sheets.

It was almost midday when Mrs Griffin, carrying a tray, woke Maggie. She drew the curtains and plumped the pillows, treating her like royalty.

And Maggie made the most of it. Here she was living on Max Jordan's terms and by Max Jordan's rules. Never in all her adult life had she surrendered so totally to another person, and yet somewhere in that act of submission she found the very thing she craved. Something about it gave her a huge thrill, and yet something about it troubled her to the core. With Max all life changed, the truths she had held so dear for so long altered and contorted in such a surreal world.

After she'd eaten Mrs Griffin returned and helped her dress, apply her make-up and brush her hair. An hour later, dressed in a cream silk basque with wired cups that displayed her breasts like ripe fruit, cream stockings and high heels, Maggie went downstairs. Catching sight of herself in a mirror she saw the face and body of a beautiful courtesan.

In the sitting room Max was busy at his desk, papers spread out in front of him. He looked up fleetingly, barely seeming to register her as she walked into the room. She hoped he would say something, compliment her appearance, but he merely indicated she should kneel at his feet, the perfect slave, the elegant possession of her master.

Max had plans for Maggie. He had already arranged for the next part of her training, but it was essential she learn fully that she was the slave, not the star.

He stroked her hair, her cheek resting on his thigh. She delighted him, she was everything he could wish for, but by the same token it was important that she understood her place in the scheme of things.

'Guido will be taking care of you today,' he told her, and she looked up in surprise. 'You want to say something, slave?'

'Um, no, master,' she said, although they both knew that wasn't true.

'Good.' Max rang the bell on his desk before turning his attention back to his papers, and a few minutes later Guido appeared. As his driver crossed the room Max felt Maggie tense, but said nothing.

Maggie looked up at him, and he indicated she should stand. She did as she was told, although her eyes were wide with apprehension. Max smiled; he had the perfect cure for that.

Guido slipped a blindfold over her eyes, gripped her arm and led her away.

Max dropped the papers back into his desk; time for the show to begin.

Maggie tried not to let her fear show, instinct telling her that Guido would take advantage of the slightest sign of weakness. He led her out of the sitting room, that much she could guess, and then across the hall and down some stairs to what she assumed were the kitchens, and then down yet more steps. It was nerve-wracking not being able to see and she shivered, afraid that she might lose her footing, while at the same time her mind was spiralling away at the prospect of what might follow.

As they turned a corner the air became cooler and slightly musty.

'Nearly there,' Guido informed her, and Maggie could hear the mixture of amusement and anticipation in his voice as they moved along a damp and chilly passage.

'W-where are we going?' she asked anxiously.

He sniggered. 'That's for me to know and you to find out.'

The floor under her feet was cold now, and the muffled sound of their voices made her sense the ceiling was low and the walls close around them.

'Here we are,' said Guido, and Maggie swung round to try and track his voice as he let go of her and moved away. 'Relax,' he said. 'I'm not going to leave you. It'll all be so much easier if you don't resist me, although you must know that by now. Do as you're told and you'll be fine.' As he spoke he took one of her hands and snapped a cuff around her wrist, pulling it out to one side and fastening it to something that held her arm parallel to the floor. He did the same with the other and Maggie fought to suppress her panic.

'My, what a pretty sight you are,' he mused, running his hands over her breasts, tweaking her nipples. Maggie squealed at the sudden pain, and with an open palm he slapped first one and then the other, making her gasp with surprise. He slapped each breast again, harder this time.

'So very pretty,' he drawled. 'I really enjoyed watching you with Freya. She's some piece of work, isn't she?' As he spoke he nudged her legs apart and fastened a spreader bar between her ankles.

'You're going to enjoy today,' he told her conversationally. 'Max has arranged something special for you.'

'What do you mean?' she asked.

He said no more, and the next sound she heard was his retreating footsteps and the sound of the door opening and closing.

'Guido?' she called anxiously. Hadn't he said he wouldn't leave her alone? 'Guido?' she called again into the ominous silence.

'Guido?' she called more earnestly, increasingly unsettled by her chilling solitude, but still there was no response of any kind. She tried to sense what was going on. The minutes ticked by slowly. She pulled on her restraints, aware even as she tugged at them that it was pointless. She became more anxious and her pulse quickened as panic again threatened to overwhelm her.

And then, just when she thought she could bear it no longer, she heard the door open again. Maggie had no idea who it was – Guido returning, or Max. Her emotions teetered between relief and trepidation. As she strained to pick up any clues as to the identity of the presence, she could just discern the movement of feet and whisper of male voices.

'H-hello?' she stuttered. 'Who is it? Master? Guido?

Is that you?'

No one answered, and Maggie tugged desperately on the restraints, twisting her wrists, trying to loosen the cuffs that held her tight.

'Is there anyone there?' she cried again, a little louder this time, at last provoking a response.

'For God's sake gag her,' ordered a male voice she didn't recognise, and then she heard footsteps and someone moving closer. Something round and hard was pushed into her mouth and straps tied tight at the back of her head. It was a ball-gag. Maggie let out a wail of apprehension. Now she couldn't speak or see, but she could still hear and her body froze as a voice whispered in her ear.

'Hello, Maggie,' it said. 'Your master tells us that you need to be used like a proper slave should be.'

Maggie strained hard against the cuffs.

'I'm sure an arrogant little bitch like you has fantasies of more than one man taking you at a time? Don't you, eh? And that's what we're here for. To make you beg for mercy and beg for more. How do you like the idea of that, eh, Maggie?'

As the voice continued to taunt soft tendrils stroked across her breasts and stomach, the touch sensual yet alarming. Maggie groaned behind the gag as her nipples responded, tightening. She shook her head in denial, trying to say no to the cruel goading, then a stinging lash across her breasts made her sex tighten and the moan from behind the gag become a wild sob. More lashes cut across her breasts, buttocks, thighs and belly. Maggie couldn't hold back, she cried and then screamed into the gag, struggling against the cuffs and spreader bar.

Just when she thought she could take no more her tormentor leant close. 'A little word of warning,

Maggie,' he whispered sharply. 'You are our plaything today. Max says we can do exactly what we want to you. And trust me, whatever we want to do to you, we will do. Although if you do what you're told we might just let you go when we've finished with you. But if not you might find yourself tied down here for quite some time.'

Maggie shrieked again as six hard strikes of a cane cut across her buttocks. She tried to force herself to stop struggling, her chest heaving as she tried to catch her breath.

Hands began working their way over her body, touching and molesting with callous intensity. Fingers slid inside her wet sex, finding and then circling the hardening ridge of her clitoris, while another eased into her bottom making her wriggle and sob in protest. As she tried to pull away from them a hungry mouth closed over one of her breasts, sucking and biting the nipple, then another mouth started suckling the other, while two pairs of hands mauled between her parted thighs from the front and from the rear.

Maggie struggled to breathe, saliva trickling around the ball-gag and down her chin. She moaned, frightened and anxious, and yet against all the odds she secretly began to enjoy the crude attentions. As if sensing her growing arousal the mouths pulled away.

She sighed, but any sense of relief was misplaced and premature.

'Enjoying it, aren't you, sweetheart?' the voice drooled salaciously. There was a moment's fumbling between her tensed thighs, she held her breath, wondering what was coming next, and then something thrust up inside her without prelude. Maggie cried out with shock as her body opened in its path, and then again as someone gripped her breasts and pinched her nipples tight with a set of cold metal clamps. The pleasure and pain combination was almost unbearable. Her sex began contracting while the thick dildo thrust without compassion in and out of her.

Maggie felt her body spasm, she couldn't hold back. It was all too much. She bit down on the gag as a fierce orgasm swept through her, her body arching as her sex closed tight around the dildo. Still gasping, still in the throws of her climax, the dildo was wrenched out and she moaned gratefully as a rigid penis slid slowly up into her vacant cunt. At the same time something smaller and slimmer was eased into her bottom, a finger slick with lubrication, and then retreated and a cock nudged up to take its place. Maggie sobbed deliriously as it embedded itself in her tight rear passage. Her mind protested but her rogue body seemed only too eager to cooperate. There was no way this was possible... no way...

The stranger screwing her arse eased his meaty erection slowly but determinedly further and further inside her. Maggie thought she would faint with pleasure and shame, writhing between the two naked men.

She sobbed pitifully, but her muffled protests were met with grunts and curses of pleasure as the two men began to find a mutual rhythm, driving in and out of their victim, sandwiched between them, tied, gagged and stretched open for them.

'Want to swap places?' rumbled the man who'd spoken previously, and with that they both withdrew, shuffled around her, exchanged places, then eased back deep inside her and continued fucking.

Maggie slumped between them, wanting it to be over. She was raw with a heady mixture of pain and pleasure. The two men began moving more erratically, fucking her with ever more urgency. She heard one gasp, and despite her fatigue her head rolled back and she shuddered with a violent orgasm as she felt the hot release of semen deep, deep inside her cunt.

'Oh fuck!' snorted the man behind her, feverishly kissing her neck and shoulder, pulling her back onto him as he thrust his cock fully up her arse, his sperm erupting deep. 'Oh, that feels so fucking *good*,' he groaned coarsely, wearily.

Sandwiched between her captors, Maggie struggled to catch her breath while their panting bodies ground hot and sweaty against her. Gradually they both withdrew, leaving her shivering and empty, listening to the muffled whisperings of her two unseen lovers. Was lover the right word? Or was assailant more appropriate?

Firm hands unfastened the gag and Maggie stretched her jaw thankfully. Other hands released the nipple clamps.

But if she had hoped to be set free she was mistaken. After a few moments the voices receded and once again she hung in the restraints straining to hear any clues as to what would happen next.

Max Jordan was the last to leave the cellar. Although he hadn't taken part in any of the activities he could almost feel the tight grip of Maggie's sex closing around his cock, imagine the way her body felt as she writhed against the twin cocks that had impaled her. He smiled and climbed the stairs back up to the sitting room, wholly delighted with his latest acquisition.

'Well, well, well,' said a familiar voice, breaking into Maggie's reverie, and she stiffened as Guido ran a hand over her aching breasts. 'Quite a show you put on there,' he said. 'And look at you now, you dirty little whore.' His finger traced the course of the semen trickling down her legs. 'Look at you – something to be used and then discarded.'

He ran a finger up to her sex and then drew it across her lips. 'I know what whores are for,' he went on, unfastening her arms so that she slumped to the floor on her hands and knees. He caught hold of her hair and Maggie shrieked in protest, but still fastened to the spreader-bar she couldn't get away from him.

She heard the zip on Guido's trousers and knew exactly what was coming next. She heard him crouching, and then from behind he drove his cock into her soaking sex, forcing it deep into her until she cried out. 'Fuck me, you dirty little bitch,' he snorted, driving deeper still and jerking her back by her hair.

'Even after the fucking those two just gave you, you're still nice and tight,' Guido sniggered. 'Max was right about you; you really are a complete slut.'

An instant later Guido gasped, she felt him buck and then he jerked once, twice and came in a pulsing eruption, flooding her sex with his warm seed. He held on to her for support for a few moments, and then hauling her to her feet pulled off the blindfold. She blinked in the dim light of the cellar, but didn't make a sound as he unfastened her ankles, peeled the grimy basque off her and led her to a small shower area off the main cellar. He watched as she washed, eyes still bright with avarice and desire, and she tried not to catch his eye. Wasn't it enough that Max allowed him to use her as and when he wanted, or was there more?

Once she was dry, and completely naked except for her collar, Guido led her back upstairs. As they approached the sitting room Maggie heard voices from within and froze. One of them she knew was the voice from the cellar, but the other one sounded equally familiar.

'What is it?' Guido goaded. 'Don't tell me you're shy.' He opened the sitting room door and Maggie's worst fears were confirmed. Max was playing host, handing out drinks, an unknown man sitting in an armchair sipping one, and by the window, holding and empty crystal glass, she saw to her complete horror stood Mike, Kay's boyfriend!

Max smiled broadly. 'Ah, excellent,' he said enthusiastically. 'Maggie, Mike would like another scotch and soda. See to it, please.'

Feeling utterly shell-shocked Maggie did as he ordered, and as she handed Mike his drink he smiled smugly at her.

'You see, Maggie,' he said, 'I told you I knew someone you'd like to meet.'

From across the room Max interrupted the tense silence that followed Mike's arrogant boast. 'Come here, Maggie,' he said, and indicated the floor beside him, and totally humiliated she did exactly as she was told and knelt at his feet. 'On all fours, I think,' he added. 'We want to see your marks.'

After a perfunctory examination Max nodded and indicated she should stand. The men, it seemed, had some business to conduct. Maggie served them more drinks and snacks as and when required, all the time aware of their eyes on her body. And when she wasn't needed she knelt at Max's feet, the epitome of submission, although all the while her mind was racing.

Max, when engrossed in discussions, toyed idly with her, and it seemed there was no part of her and no time when she was not his property. As the afternoon headed into evening Max suggested they retire to the dining room for dinner.

At the door he kissed her on the lips. 'Well done,' he said, and the two simple words made her heart leap. 'I want you help serve my guests their meal,' he added. 'And then you can go to your room and eat. I'll have Mrs Griffin bring a tray of something up for you.' His expression suddenly hardened. 'And when you've eaten you will go and kneel by my bed until I come up.'

'Yes, master,' she yielded meekly, and realised that for the first time she truly meant the words, that in all senses Max Jordan truly was her master.

Chapter Eight

Sitting at her desk in the office of the magazine where she worked, staring at the computer screen, Maggie struggled to make sense of the articles she had been working on the week before. It felt as if the words and thoughts came from a different life, written by a different person. In fact, it felt almost as if she had woken up inside a dream.

'Maggie?' She looked up without really thinking to find Simon standing beside her desk. Couldn't the bloody man take a hint? But before she could say anything he smiled at her crookedly, giving her an odd sense of déjà vu – hadn't this been the moment that had driven her to seek out Max Jordan?

'I just came over to say that I think I owe you an apology,' he said, surprising her with his unexpected display of contrition. 'I shouldn't have told the world and his wife that you were coming out for dinner with me last week. It was tactless of me, and... well, lunging at you wasn't the most gentlemanly thing I could have done either.' He paused thoughtfully. 'The thing is, I value your friendship, Maggie, and even if you're not interested in me in a romantic way, which I do understand, I'd hate to lose you as a friend.'

Maggie managed to put on a smile. It was a very big thing for him to say, under the circumstances. 'It's all right, Simon,' she said graciously. 'And thank you.'

'There's just one more thing...' he went on, and Maggie sighed, knowing there had to be something else to it. 'I wondered if you could do me a favour.'

'A favour?'

He nodded.

'What sort of a favour, Simon?'

'Would you come out to dinner with me tonight?'

Maggie laughed. She had to admire the cheek of the man. 'That isn't a favour, that's a date.'

'No, no it's not, honestly,' he insisted defensively. 'The thing is, my department is entertaining some very influential clients this evening. I've already roped in three or four of the staff, but to be honest I could do with all the help I can get.' He paused and tried out his pretty feeble little boy lost expression on her. 'I really could do with your help, Maggie. I really could.'

She studied his eyes closely, and then smiled. She still felt a little guilty about the dinner date at the *Neptune*, and came to a decision. 'All right,' she said after a few seconds, 'just as long as you understand that it's not a date, okay?'

Simon grinned, looking mightily relieved – or pleased with himself. 'Okay,' he beamed, and just then a courier approached Maggie's desk carrying a huge bouquet of snow-white Arum lilies.

'Maggie Howard?' he asked, correctly addressing her. 'These are for you.' And she accepted them, somewhat taken aback. They were astonishingly beautiful, if slightly macabre.

Simon looked at her and then at the flowers. 'Someone die?' he blurted with his usual lack of tact.

Maggie opened the card and read the words inside. 'A little something to mark the end of your old life and beginning of the new. Check your email. The master.' She felt her cheeks blush. 'You could say that,' she said to Simon. 'Just someone's idea of a joke, that's all.' Hastily she tucked the card into her bag.

'We'll go straight from work, then,' Simon said.

'I'm sorry?'

'To dinner,' he qualified. 'I've booked an early reservation at *Fernando's*; our clients have got a long way to travel home.'

Maggie groaned. 'I'll have to nip out at lunchtime and get something to wear,' she told him, wishing she'd never agreed to help him out.

'Why?' he asked cheesily. 'You look great as you are.'

Maggie looked down at her faded jeans and black silk blouse. She had complied with Max's edict about wearing no underwear, but he had kind of fudged the rules; after all, he hadn't said anything about trousers or generous fitting blouses so that no one would notice. 'Only a man would say that,' she said scornfully.

Simon shrugged. 'About half-six, then?' he confirmed, and Maggie nodded. No point in trying to backtrack now.

As soon as he was gone she logged on to the Internet, and as she waited for her email to appear she pondered the prospect of dinner with Simon. She didn't really want to go out with him again, but it would probably mean she at least missed seeing Kay, and the inevitable embarrassment that encounter would bring.

Maggie shivered, thinking about Mike and the events of the weekend as her master's address appeared on one of the incoming emails. It had occurred to her that Kay almost certainly didn't know about Mike and his clandestine activities. Maybe she thought he kept his sadist streak just for her. How could she possibly face her lodger and friend ever again, knowing what she now knew?

Maggie opened Max's email. All there was, typed centre page, was an address in a nearby town – no date, no time, just the address and a set of instructions on how to dress. Short skirt, blouse, hold-up stockings, no underwear. Maggie smiled; it was almost the kind of outfit she could wear to dinner with Simon if she chose something subtle.

She stared at the screen, unsure whether to email or ring to ask Max for further instructions. Her instincts told her it was a test. She glanced at the lilies and decided to wait. A man who knew she was at the office rather than at home left nothing to chance. She'd have the information she needed as and when he decided she should.

'Maggie?' She instantly recognised Max's voice on the mobile, and trembled slightly. The last thing she'd expected was for the phone he'd given her to ring while she was out with Simon's clients.

'Be at the address I sent you at eight tonight,' he told her. 'You have your instructions; you know what to wear.'

Across the room a waiter served wine and fruit juice to Simon's corporate guests.

'I – I'm sorry, I'm busy at the moment...' she blustered. 'I'm helping at a business dinner with Simon from accounts.'

'Really?' He didn't sound amused. 'Well get out of it. Unless, of course, you want to displease me? Or is this disobedience? Do you want to be punished?'

'No, master...' she said urgently, her pulse quickening.

'Good, in that case I will see you at eight. I want your help with the training of another slave. I'll be expecting you, the door will be unlocked, come straight in. And try to remember all you've been taught, Maggie. Don't disappoint me...' His voice was low and even, and before Maggie had the chance to reply he hung up.

Just then Simon beckoned her over, and she really didn't know what to do for the best. 'This place is great for a function room, isn't it?' he said, looking tense, clearly keen to make a good impression on his clients. 'And the food is superb.'

She nodded. 'It's very nice, Simon,' she agreed, 'but I'm afraid I'm going to have to leave you to it; something's come up.'

He stared at her, looking agitated. 'Leave?' he whispered furiously. 'But why? We've only just got here. I thought you said you'd help me out.' She could see he was angry, and justifiably so.

'I'm really sorry, Simon,' she said, thinking on her feet. 'But I've just had a call from an interview I've been chasing for weeks. They're only in the country for a few days but the PR guy says they can see me tonight – another magazine has been bumped off the A list. I'm so sorry.'

Simon didn't look very convinced. 'So who is this mystery celebrity, then?' he challenged.

'Look, I really can't talk about it,' she fudged. 'I've just got to go. I'm sorry.'

He sighed. 'Okay, if you must.'

Maggie smiled, the knot in her stomach easing. 'I owe you one,' she said, and with the first hurdle out of the way she slipped into the cloakroom and took off the white lacy knickers and bra she'd bought at lunchtime, and looked at herself in the mirror. It wouldn't take long to get ready. A little more make-up and a button or two more undone on her new white blouse, a little more perfume and she was ready. She smiled at her reflection, aware of the way the outline of her nipples showed through the thin fabric.

'Wow,' said Simon as she reappeared. 'You look great. I hope this mystery celeb is worth it.'

Maggie reddened. 'Were you waiting for me?' she asked.

'I just came to ask if you'd like me to drive you to the interview?' he said. 'After all, your car is back at the office.'

Maggie shook her head. 'No, it's all right,' she declined the offer, 'I've arranged for a taxi. And besides, this is your bash, you're the host, Simon, you can hardly leave.'

Ten minutes later, settled in the back of a cab, she wondered what Max meant about helping him out with another slave. Did he mean Beau, perhaps, or someone else? As she allowed her imagination to run riot she felt a familiar stirring deep in the pit of her tummy, a hot tendril of arousal surging up through her like a lightening bolt. She made a point of keeping her eyes lowered in case the driver could see the desire sparkling in them.

Shortly before eight the taxi drew up outside the address Max had given her. As she climbed out into the anonymous suburban street the evening air touched her nakedness beneath the short skirt.

The taxi driver seemed to sense her apprehension. 'You going to be all right on your own here, love?' he asked as Maggie paid him.

She nodded, not trusting herself to speak, holding her

coat tight, certain that somehow he knew that beneath it she was dressed for Max Jordan, as he had decreed she should be.

She shivered, watching the taillights of the taxi disappear around the corner, letting the sense of excitement and isolation thrill her. She drew a calming breathed, amazed at the change that had come over her since Max's phone call.

The house he'd directed her to was a modern suburban villa on an executive estate, hidden away behind neatly trimmed shrubs and an expanse of manicured lawn. Maggie made her way up the drive, aware of her high heels crunching on the gravel.

The house was quiet as she let herself in through the front door. The hall was tastefully furnished but at the same time oddly featureless, as if styled from the pages of a Sunday magazine. Maggie hesitated, wondering what to do next, when she heard a familiar voice.

'Up here,' Max called.

She slipped off her coat and checked her appearance in the hall mirror, tucking the white blouse tighter into her skirt, pulling the thin fabric taut over her breasts so her nipples showed through. She climbed the stairs tentatively. There was only one door open on the landing, light spilling from it. Taking a deep breath she slipped into the bedroom, and gasped. In the luxuriously furnished room was a naked woman, tied facedown on the bed, a pillow under her hips, her raised buttocks crisscrossed with blotchy welts. Maggie stared, there was something terribly familiar about her, and then she realised with horror it was her lodger, Kay!

Her face was turned to one side, her long blonde hair fanned out across the white pillows, a black blindfold covering her eyes. She was breathing hard.

Max Jordan stood to one side of the bed, fully

dressed, a black leather riding-crop held loosely at his side.

'Come over here,' he ordered, and as Maggie got close he grabbed her hair and pulled her to him with a brutal ferocity and gave her a crushing kiss. Maggie gasped, she could feel the heat in him and his animal arousal induced by the whipping he'd given Kay. He pressed his fingers between her legs, under her skirt, his fingers demanding entry, prising into Maggie's already wet sex. She sighed with shameful pleasure.

He pulled away from the kiss, grabbed the front of her new blouse and ripped it open. There was no place for subtlety, and clenching his jaw he tore it away from her body completely, heedless of ruining her new garment.

Maggie cried out in shock, yet at the same time felt her body respond to the hungry assault. He leered and swooped to capture a nipple between his teeth, biting hard enough to make her cry out with pain. She began to writhe against him, astonished by her own hunger.

'Please, master,' she begged, barely aware of her own words, 'please fuck me.'

'Oh, so keen already?' he said scornfully. 'Not yet, my beautiful little slave, not yet. We have a long night ahead of us.' He turned her away from him. 'Give me your hands.'

Maggie did as she was told, aware of the paradox of fear and desire, aware that only a short while earlier such a request would have had her screaming for help. She felt the cold bite of the handcuffs snapping shut around her wrists, and then the light receding as Max tied a blindfold over her eyes.

'You look magnificent,' he said, hands on her shoulders, pushing her down to her knees. She heard the sound of his trouser zip being lowered, felt his hand as it cupped her chin, holding her head still, and then the feel of his smooth helmet demanding entry to her mouth. Maggie opened for him, at that moment wanting nothing more than to give her master total pleasure. Kneeling in an act of worship, relishing the feel, the smell and the taste of his cock as it slid over her lips, she sighed with pure pleasure.

'Suck me,' he ordered, and then held himself still. She obeyed, moving her head and using her lips and tongue to please him.

'That's it... that's very good,' he panted softly. 'Good girl, that feels very good.'

Maggie moaned her reply as the taste of his growing excitement filled her mouth.

'You know what you are, don't you?' he went on. 'You're my dirty little whore, my little slave... my slut. What other kind of a girl would abandon her boyfriend at my call, and hurry across town to let her body be used by another man?' He began to thrust deeper into her mouth. 'Mmmmm, yes... only a slut would let herself be used like this, on her knees, hands tied behind her back. Mmmmm, that's it, suck harder you dirty little cunt. What sort of girl are you, Maggie? Letting her mouth be fucked... and *wanting* it. You do want it, don't you, Maggie? Hmmm?' Max paused, pulling his cock almost out of her mouth.

She groaned, feeling robbed, and then eased forward to draw his cock back deep into her mouth as the riding-crop licked at the cheeks of her backside.

'Oh yes, that's it... that's it you dirty little slut. Suck harder, harder now.'

Max's crude words and Maggie's helplessness threatened to consume her. She pressed her thighs tight together, trying desperately to find a way to her own orgasm. Behind them she could hear Kay begging to be released, begging to be allowed to orgasm too. Max's fingers tightened in Maggie's hair, holding her head still as he began to fuck her mouth in earnest.

'Have you any idea how you look?' he grunted thickly as his pleasure grew. It was almost too much for him. Maggie Howard kneeling in front of him, the excitement of Kay's beating fresh in his mind. He gasped, struggling to hold on, struggling to hold back. He knew that both Maggie and Kay were desperate for release. Maggie was trembling, aching to touch herself as she sucked him. She looked every inch the perfect slut, her pretty tits available to be fondled and used, her short skirt bunching up around her waist, her cunt wet, almost totally exposed, waiting for a cock... any cock. He threw back his head and cried out with pleasure as the spunk pulsed up and out of his body and into Maggie's sucking mouth. Behind them on the bed Kay wailed in fury and frustration because she couldn't bring on her own orgasm. Jet after jet spewed from his cock, filling Maggie's mouth as she tried valiantly to swallow it all. When almost totally spent he held her head still and thrust into her welcoming mouth, using her purely for his pleasure, prolonging his ejaculation and the last of the bliss.

As the final tremor dissipated his wilting cock plopped from Maggie's mouth. She didn't move, waiting like a good slave for whatever was to follow. Max bent down and cupped her wet sex.

'Please, master,' she whimpered, 'please make me come.'

Max smiled. It was far too soon for that. From the cabinet by the bed he took out a small vibrator and eased it into her sex. She almost fell forward against him as he slid it into her, and set it vibrating at a slow throb. Maggie pushed down onto the carpet, shamelessly struggling to fuck herself on the plastic column.

'There you are, my little whore, that should keep you happy for a while,' he mused. 'Although you have a lot more work to do before you are allowed to orgasm tonight.'

The doorbell rang and Max left the bedroom. Maggie felt a little rush of panic. She could hear the sounds of Max welcoming someone and then strained to pick out individual voices. No, there was more than one other voice, more than two, but how many? She could hear them climbing the stairs, drawing nearer, and then they fell silent.

Maggie blushed furiously under the blindfold, knowing that whomever Max had invited to join him in the bedroom was taking in the extraordinary sight of her and Kay.

Nothing was said, but she sensed people crowding around, and picked out the distinctive sounds of clothes being shed. She could also sense the growing excitement and anticipation.

She felt someone move close to her face and then heard Max's distinctive Irish lilt. 'Now, my little slut, do you remember why I told you I wanted you here tonight?'

'Yes, to help you with Kay, master,' she answered clearly.

Max's fingers nipped her nipples, just hard enough for there to be a little pain, making her wince beneath the blindfold. 'No, I told you what was going to happen to Kay, didn't I?'

'You said you wanted my help with the training of another slave.'

'Good, and you'll start helping right now.' Maggie felt his hand on the back of her head, pressing her forward, and then her cheek was brushed by another stiff cock. 'Open your mouth, my little slut,' he whispered. 'That's what you're here for tonight. I want you to make all these cocks hard. Make them ready to fuck Kay.'

Maggie's futile response was instantly muffled as the cock moved across her cheek and thrust deep into her mouth. It felt different to Max's, and a tremor of excitement rippled through her body as she realised what was happening, reduced to a sexual aid for men who cared nothing about who she was, only what she represented: pure pleasure without a name or a face. The idea of being reduced to nothing more than a sexual toy made her shiver. The man standing over her pushed deeper, making her work to please him, and Maggie let go, abandoning herself to the pleasure, to the sensation of each new cock as the men took turns in her mouth, and along with it was the knowledge that each of the cocks would soon be thrust into Kay's prone body. She shivered, imagining her lodger being used over and over again.

Each man took his turn in her mouth, using it, enjoying it, panting huskily as she sucked until they were rigid. But each one pulled away before they ejaculated.

'I want you to get up now,' Max eventually said, removing the dildo, Maggie shuddering as it slipped out of her pulsating cunt. He pulled her to her feet, guiding her forward, unfastening the cuffs. Then with him holding her hand she was led across the room and cringed with shock as her fingertips were lowered to Kay's smooth calves.

'Here,' said Max, pressing a tube of something into her palm. 'My friends have come to play, Maggie. They're all going to fuck Kay now, one right after the other, some in her arse, some in her cunt, some in her mouth. You've made their cocks nice and hard for her, and now I think you'd better make her ready for them, don't you?'

Maggie felt Kay tremble under her fingers as she heard the instructions. 'I can't, I don't know how...' she said. The only female she'd ever been intimate with was Freya, and on that occasion Freya had taken the lead. And worse still, Kay was her friend, someone she shared her house with.

'Maggie,' Max warned, his tone threatening, and she knew that disobeying him was a bad idea. So slowly, fearfully, she slipped forward onto the bed and ran her hands up the backs of Kay's bound and parted legs, seeking the girl's sex.

'Please,' Maggie begged, 'please may I see what I'm doing?'

'Not yet, Maggie,' he denied her. 'I just want you to touch her, to feel her body. Now do as you're told or I'll take the crop to you and to her. Hold out your hand.'

Max squeezed a greasy cream onto her raised fingers, and she obediently and blindly lubricated between Kay's beaten buttocks, surprised when the girl lifted her hips to her tentative touch, actually twisting beneath her fingers, the lubricant coating her tight anus. Instinctively Maggie slipped a single finger inside, and then ventured another, and Kay began to moan and thrust against her, trying to work the fingers deeper still.

Maggie imagined the men gathered around the bed, watching the two of them together, lining up to use Kay's trussed body. Maggie's fingers slid deeper, fucking Kay while her other hand fumbled between her own legs, gasping as her fingers touched her throbbing pleasure bud. The men were urging her on, and she could feel her orgasm drawing closer and closer...

'Stop!' Max's voice cut through the air as the riding-crop swiped viciously across Maggie's buttocks. Panting, groaning, no more than seconds away from her orgasm, she fell still, trembling, denied the closeness of release. He guided her down off the bed to kneel on the floor at the foot of it, and then he handcuffed her to the metal frame.

She felt his warm breath on her neck as he bent over to whisper in her ear. 'Do you know what my friends are going to do now, Maggie?'

She could say nothing.

'Do you know?' he pressed, and she nodded. 'Then tell me, little one, what do you think they are going to do now?'

'They're going to fuck her, master,' she said.

'And where are they going to fuck her, Maggie?'

'In her cunt, in her arse, in her mouth,' she whispered, horrified by the crude words coming from her mouth and lurid images forming in her head.

'Yes, they're going to fuck her, Maggie,' he confirmed. 'They're going to fuck her until she screams with pleasure.' Max ran a finger down her spine, and she shivered. 'And then, my dear, they are going to fuck you.'

Before she could fully absorb the implications of what he said she felt the bed move under her hands and realised that more than anything else she wanted to be able to see what was happening. The mattress strained and suddenly Kay was begging.

'Oh yes, yes, please fuck me, please, please fuck me…' the words breaking into a deluge of incoherent sobs as the bed began to move rhythmically. Maggie strained against the cuffs, hungry to see, desperate to watch.

It was more than she could bear – the sounds, the movements, all contriving to drive her crazy with anticipation and desire. Some part of her, she was horrified to realise, was desperate to see Kay being fucked and used.

She was aware of hands on her hips, and knew Max was behind her, watching Kay being fucked. 'Tell me, master, please,' she begged. 'Tell me what you see.'

He sniggered, stroked her bottom with the crop, and then administered a stinging blow across it. 'Listen, my dear, listen to them, and imagine her being fucked by my friends!'

Maggie sighed with frustration, and heard the man fucking Kay begin to pant and gasp. He was close to the brink, ready to explode inside her body, and then Maggie knew he was there. She heard him groan, heard him grunt, and in her mind she saw him thrusting stiffly into Kay's helpless body, saw his whole frame tensing as he emptied his balls in the girl's available sex.

But it was far from over. There was movement again, the bed rocking, another man clambering onto it, thrusting deep into Kay. She moaned again, moaning as he stretched her, used her, flesh slapping flesh, faster and faster. Behind the blindfold Maggie closed her eyes tight shut. Kay began to come too, making the mattress buck as the man riding her giggled victoriously and ejaculated inside her.

Then Maggie felt Max thrusting into her, deep into her soaking sex. She sighed, relishing the penetration, his hands gripping her hips, pulling her back onto him, straining against the cuffs that held her to the gyrating bed.

Her mind was alight with sounds and smells; Kay's insistent cries as she came over and over again; a man telling the trussed girl how he was going to fuck her, then his triumphant expletives as he came too; the bed-frame shaking under her hands; Max's stout cock thrusting deep into her body; her own pleasure so intense she thought she might faint.

At that moment Max pulled the blindfold off, and the salacious images on the bed did drive Maggie over the edge into a shuddering orgasm.

Max leant forward and withdrew his unspent erection, whispering in her ear, 'I can't keep you all to myself, that would be selfish. What sort of a host would that make me?'

He rose and stepped away, and Maggie felt an anonymous hand rummaging between her thighs, groping her vacant cunt, a rampant cock brushing her buttocks, and she closed her eyes.

Chapter Nine

When they got back to Maggie's house Guido opened the car door for her. She was too tired to speak, other than to wish him a perfunctory goodnight. Her mind and her body were totally exhausted as she fumbled for her front door key.

'Well, well, well, just look who's here,' said a familiar voice as she slipped the key into the lock. Slightly bemused she looked around and was astonished to see Simon standing there in the shadows.

'What are you doing here at this time of night?' she asked, unable to keep the surprise out of her voice.

'Now, there's a nice thing to say to someone who was concerned about your welfare,' he said sarcastically. 'I thought the very least I could do was make sure you got home safe and sound after you deserted me like that. You could invite me in, for being so considerate. How did your interview go? What did they do, ask you to stay on for the after-show party or something?'

Maggie tried to gather her thoughts and her alibi. 'Something like that,' she said hastily. 'It was okay. It was fine.'

'So, was that their driver?' he probed. 'You must have made a good impression to wangle yourself a ride home.' Simon nodded towards the road, although Guido had long since gone.

Maggie gave a noncommittal shrug and opened the front door.

'You look tired; are you sure you're all right?' he asked.

'Look, I'm fine, Simon,' she said frostily. 'I'm touched that you came to check up on me, but to be perfectly honest all I want to do now is fall into bed.' She looked at him, and he looked crestfallen. 'Okay, tell you what, why don't you come in and have a quick coffee,' she relented against her better judgement, his expression instantly brightening.

'Great!' he beamed, following her inside. 'Thanks, Maggie.'

'Actually, Simon, maybe this isn't such a good idea, I really need a shower,' she said, once they were in the hall.

'Don't let me stop you. I'm quite domesticated you know. You go and have your shower and leave the coffee to me.'

Upstairs Maggie dropped the ruins of her new clothes into the bin and looked at her body in the mirror.

Her nipples were red and sore from bite marks and far too much attention. Her bottom was striped from the crop and her sex was sore. She closed her eyes, remembering the frenzied animal heat of the men as they took her again and again. She shivered. Until meeting Max she would never have believed herself capable of such behaviour.

Feeling increasingly tired she set the shower to hot and stepped gratefully beneath the refreshing torrent. The more she thought about it, the more she felt it had been a mistake to let Simon in. There was no way she wanted to be sociable with him; all she wanted was to crawl into the warmth and comfort of her bed...

Maggie shrieked as Simon, naked, squeezed into the shower with her. 'What do you think you're playing at?' she snapped furiously, incredulously, trying to cover herself with her arms. 'Get out of here this instant!'

But Simon just grinned at her. 'Oh come on, Maggie, stop playing hard to get,' he said infuriatingly. 'You know I've fancied you for ages. And all that crap about not fancying me? I'm not fooled by that for an instant.'

Was he drunk? 'Simon,' she said, trying to control her outrage, 'get out of my shower, my bathroom, and my house, now. Please, before you do something we both regret. Go now and I'll never say anything more about it.'

Simon giggled inanely, and then cupping her face he kissed her aggressively, one hand straying down to maul her breasts while a knee pressed determinedly between her thighs.

'Come on, Maggie, don't be so coy,' he growled, breaking away from the kiss. 'I know you really fancy me, and besides, you're all on your own. I know you're gagging for it, a girl in your position, no one to snuggle up to at night. Come on, you know you want to. I thought maybe you'd like a little bit of rough.'

He kissed her again, trying to force his tongue into her mouth, making her squirm back against the wet tiles in horror. 'I'll scream and wake Kay!' she spluttered, managing to push him away.

Simon's eyes darkened menacingly. 'Nice try,

Maggie, but I've already looked in her room and she's not home,' he said ominously. 'There's just you and me, and this…' His face rubbed against hers as he kissed her forehead, almost paternally, while with one hand he brushed his engorged cock against her belly.

'Simon, get out,' she implored weakly, physically and mentally drained from the night's exertions. 'Please, just get out and let's forget this ever happened…'

Before she could stop him he pressed her back against the tiles, sneering at her words as he forced her legs wider apart with his knee, his breath laden with alcohol. She started to struggle, knowing there was no reasoning with him, but he merely tutted sarcastically and grabbed her hair, pulling her face within inches of his.

'Come on, darling,' he gloated, 'we both know you'll love it. Just relax, take it easy and enjoy a real man. I'm not going to hurt you, just give you the fucking you need to loosen you up a little.'

Maggie felt her anger flare, but he was too strong and easily quelled her resistance. She tried to push him away again, pressing her clenched fists to his chest, but he was unrelenting.

'Simon, stop,' she begged. 'You're drunk, and I know when you sober up you'll regret this… Simon, please…'

As she tried to knee him he dragged her out of the shower cubicle and threw her to the bathroom floor. Instantly he was upon her, giving her no respite, pinning her to the tiles with one hand while guiding his cock into her with the other.

'There we are, sweetheart,' he grunted. 'You know you love it really. Now just relax while I give you the best screw you've ever had.'

Maggie mumbled wearily for him to stop, but far from stopping Simon seemed to be further inflamed by her pleas.

'Shit, that feels fantastic,' he groaned, throwing his head back. 'Oh yes, that feels bloody great. I knew you'd feel this good, Maggie. I've always known it, and now I'm really fucking you.' Snorting and grunting he began to buck and twist inside her, driving deeper and deeper, moving increasingly raggedly, and quickly he ejaculated – too quickly for his liking – while Maggie felt tears of shame running down her face as he pressed fully into her and held himself there, his groin tight between her parted thighs, his penis throbbing rhythmically as it discharged his seed deep into her body. He snorted through clenched teeth, sinewy veins standing proud in his throat, his eyes shut as he luxuriated in the triumph of at last fucking Maggie.

He collapsed onto her, feverishly raining kisses on her face and her throat in some loathsome parody of love or affection.

'Phew!' he gasped in her ear. 'Wasn't that something? I knew you wanted me all along. I knew you'd be good, too. But not that fucking good!'

Maggie stared up at the ceiling in disbelieving horror.

'Shall I go and make us that coffee now?' he asked, sliding out of her, his cock leaving a sticky trail across her trembling tummy.

'Coffee?' Maggie said quietly, unable to believe what she was hearing. 'You bastard, Simon; how could you do this to me? Get out of my house now and leave me alone.'

Simon got to his feet, his expression smug. 'Don't be silly, Maggie. You invited me in for coffee; I didn't twist your arm. You wanted me to fuck you. That's why you came up here on the pretext of wanting a shower, rather conveniently leaving the bathroom door unlocked. You wanted me to follow you up and fuck you. You just won't admit it to me, or to yourself. It's about time you did, Maggie. It's about time you did.'

For long uncomfortable seconds Simon stared down at her, gloating, then turned and left the bathroom.

She waited until she heard the front door open and close, and then crawled back into the shower and washed away any traces of his touch. The water had gone cold when she finally got out of the shower, towelled herself dry and slipped gratefully into bed.

It was almost light when Maggie heard her bedroom door open. She woke from sleep with a start and instantly tensed, terrified it might be Simon back for more.

She heard light footsteps padding across the bedroom, felt the duvet pull back, and was about to react when a familiar voice said, 'Don't worry, it's only me. I thought you might need a cuddle.'

Maggie sighed with relief and surprise. She couldn't have put it better herself. The body snuggled to her was warm and soft and belonged to her lodger. Kay was the very last person she would have expected to climb into her bed at any time, least of all tonight.

'Are you okay?' Kay whispered.

'Sort of,' said Maggie, her voice trembling with unexpected emotion. It wasn't the after-effects of the evening spent with Max and his friends that unsettled her, but Simon's unsophisticated attentions. Kay's unexpected tenderness brought tears to her eyes.

Not that Kay was to know that, and she very gently kissed Maggie, who began to respond, and eased her tongue into Maggie mouth, holding her close while her hands stroked and caressed her trembling body. As she began to relax Kay cupped Maggie's breasts, murmuring soft words of encouragement while caressing her.

Maggie shivered as Kay worked her lips over her throat and shoulders, and then lower to her breasts, her soft kisses and fingers eagerly teasing her stirring nipples. Maggie let out a long sigh, moaning with a heady mixture of uncertainty and delight. Despite her fears Kay's touch was sure and persuasive, each caress lighting a thousand tiny flares in Maggie's sleepy mind.

'Oh,' Maggie moaned as she felt trembling flutters of arousal. 'We... we can't do this,' she stammered.

'Shhhhh, it's all right,' Kay soothed, the words humming on Maggie's flesh as she sucked one of her nipples into her mouth. 'Max told me to come home and make love to you,' she confided. 'He told me to make you sing with pure pleasure. Here, touch me, Maggie. I'm here for you. I've wanted you for some time. Let me show you.' Finding Maggie's hands she guided them to her own full breasts.

The girl's skin was as soft as spun silk and warm and fluid under Maggie's fingertips, her lithe form a stunning contrast to the masculine brawn of the others. Maggie gasped at just how beautiful Kay felt, and almost without thinking she lowered her head and drew Kay's erect nipple into her mouth. The blonde moaned appreciatively and lifted herself up, pressing towards Maggie in both invitation and acceptance of her tentative caresses.

With Freya, Maggie had felt very much the slave, dominated and taken by a cruelly dominant mistress. But curled up in Kay's arms there was just intimate pleasure, two girls making love to each other in a way she had never dreamt she would find so deliciously consuming.

Kay's fingers brushed Maggie's sex, making the breath catch in her throat.

'Trust me, it'll be beautiful,' Kay murmured, taking one of Maggie's hands and gently guiding it between her own legs. Maggie made no effort to resist, but was surprised at just how wet Kay was, her sex hot and seeping creamy silk. She knew this was a present from Max Jordan, a present to them both.

Kay gently guided Maggie's kisses down over her breasts and belly to the shaven mound of her sex. As she pressed kisses to the girl's flesh, Maggie could smell Kay's excitement and feel the ripples of pleasure sifting through her body.

For a moment, lying alongside Kay, her face and lips a fraction away from Kay's fragrant quim, Maggie hesitated, nervous and unsure. She had never been attracted to her own sex, but thanks to Max Jordan all that, and much more, had changed.

'Please,' Kay whispered, lifting her hips towards Maggie's waiting mouth. 'Please kiss me.'

How could she possibly refuse? Tentatively she pressed her lips to the fleshy lips, imaging what the kiss would feel like. Beneath her the girl gasped in delight and lifted her hips to give Maggie greater access, her fingers joining Maggie's tongue, holding her sex open for Maggie's caresses. Slowly, trying hard to still her own fears and doubts as much as anything else, Maggie slipped her tongue into Kay's open sex and licked like an inquisitive kitten, her taste buds suffused by the richly oceanic flavour of Kay's excitement. She let the tip of her tongue ease across the engorged ridge of Kay's clitoris, knowing instinctively that it wouldn't take much to push her over the edge. She nibbled and lapped at the engorged bud, sucking it eagerly.

'Oh…' Kay gasped, and pulled Maggie up to straddle her face. Groaning, the lithe blonde pulled her hips down, so that Maggie had no choice but to settle her own throbbing sex onto the waiting mouth. She immediately felt herself respond to Kay's intense caresses, felt her body accepting them.

When her orgasm came an engulfing wave swept through the two of them, and Maggie trembled uncontrollably with pure pleasure. She fell into a deep and contented sleep, curled up in the other girl's arms.

When she woke in the morning Maggie was alone, fresh sunlight streaming in through the bedroom window. She lay for a few minutes letting all manner of thoughts roll through her head, trying to work out what was real and what was a dream. One by one as the events and memories of the previous evening and night unfolded, she realised that of all of them she was far more embarrassed and confused by what had happened with Simon Faraday than anything else.

Over breakfast Kay didn't mention anything. In fact, she acted as if nothing had happened between them at all.

Fortunately Maggie and Simon's paths didn't cross until the end of the week.

'I really need to talk to you,' he said as she parked in the office car park and hurried across the tarmac to reception. It was first thing in the morning and Maggie had no intention of lingering.

'I've got nothing I want to say to you, Simon, and if you come anywhere near me I'll call security,' she threatened, with considerably more confidence than she felt.

'Oh come on, Maggie, stop playing games with me,' he countered, and she swung round, outraged by the condescending tone of his voice.

'Playing games?' she said. 'What do you mean by

that, Simon?'

He shook his head in disbelief. 'Maggie, I know you've been on your own for quite a while, and I know what you like. You've wanted what I gave you for some time now. Don't you deny it,' he said quickly as she opened her mouth to object. 'Girls like you don't know how to ask for what they want, so you need a real man to show you. You've been giving me the come on for months, you know you have.'

She stared at him in total astonishment. Where on earth was all this patronising rubbish coming from? 'Simon, all I've ever done is be friendly towards you,' she stated, trying very hard not to lose her temper completely. 'I've never given you any encouragement whatsoever.' Why on earth was she even talking to the creep?

'What if I said I was sorry?' he said.

Maggie shook her head. 'It would mean considerably more if I thought for an instant that you meant it,' she said.

He glowered her. 'Have you ever considered that you've got some kind of sexual problem, Maggie?'

They were walking through reception, Simon scuttling along just behind her. She was beginning to get really angry, but fighting to maintain her dignity. She didn't want him to see he was getting to her. 'I don't have a *sexual* problem, Simon. The only problem I have is with you; now get out of my face.'

'I was wondering if maybe you're frigid,' he went on regardless, infuriating her, 'only most women find me very attractive?'

Maggie shook her head at the nerve and the arrogance of the man. If only he knew. She didn't bother gracing his incredible, conceited remarks with a reply, and instead stepped into a waiting lift and closed the doors in his face, shaking with rage as it smoothly started to ascend. What a bastard!

When she got to her floor and the metal doors slid aside, she was stunned to see Simon standing there in the corridor, red-faced and out of breath.

'Look, Maggie,' he wheezed, hands on hips, struggling to recover from the exertion of running up four flights of stairs, 'stop fighting me, will you. I wondered if you might be interested in spending a weekend with me in the country, that's all. A friend of mine has a lovely little cottage that we could borrow. It would be great if we could spend some time together.'

She shook her head in amazement. 'Simon, I'm only going to say this once more and then I'm going to lose my patience with you. I'm not interested in you. I've never been interested in you. I'm sorry if you think I've given you the wrong signals at any stage, but trust me, this is not some elaborate game of chase me, chase me. I genuinely don't want to go out with you. Not now, not ever. Is that perfectly clear?'

She couldn't have been more frank, but to her horror he smiled, still utterly undeterred. 'Whatever you say, Maggie.' And then he actually winked! She wanted to slap him. How could he possibly believe this was another round of her playing hard to get?

'Simon, I want you to know that I've found someone,' she said, trying a different tack, but he just shrugged.

'Funny you've only just thought to mention it, Maggie,' he said dismissively. 'But don't worry, I'm a patient man. I can wait.'

As she watched him walk away she wondered if it would ever be possible to have an ordinary relationship again, not with Simon but with any normal man. She suspected there was no way back from the place that Max Jordan had taken her, or the things he had shown and taught her so far.

Part of her was aware that this was only the beginning of her education.

The rest of the day was full and busy. Maggie opened her email, cleared her post, working quietly and effectively through the things on her desk and on the computer without being disturbed again by Simon. But as the day wore on she found it harder and harder to concentrate, wondering if and when she would hear from Max, after all it was Friday, wasn't he supposed to ring her?

Just before five she got a call from reception. 'Courier for you, Ms Howard, with a parcel. Shall we send him up or will you come down and collect it?'

Intrigued, Maggie headed downstairs to pick up what turned out to be a large flat black box tied around with an enormous silver ribbon. The security guy on reception grinned and winked. 'Looks like you're in for a good weekend, miss,' he said.

'Probably just a cake from my mother,' she joked.

The man laughed and handed her the box. On the form attached to it was the name Max Jordan in heavy typeface.

Back upstairs, safely installed behind her desk, Maggie pulled off the ribbons and then had second thoughts.

Although it was quite quiet – those who could had already left for home – maybe it wasn't such a good idea to open Max's present there. Glancing around to see if anyone was watching, she headed down to the women's cloakroom.

Once safely inside a cubicle she pulled off the wrappings. In the box was a black PVC miniskirt, a matching camisole top and high-heeled black boots –

and a card that read, *Guido will pick you up at18:00. The Master*.

It was Friday evening and the main offices were more or less empty. She could get changed and then slip out the back way down the fire escape to the car park without anyone seeing her.

Ten minutes later she stared at her reflection in the cloakroom mirror and smiled; no one who saw her in the PVC outfit would recognise the refined Maggie Howard who wrote magazine home and style articles. The vixen who looked back from the mirror had style all right, but not of the publishable kind. The hem of the tight skirt came to just below the cheeks of her bottom, and the little black top pushed her breasts together and forward, the plunging neckline barely covering her nipples, offering her breasts like ripe fruits. And the boots? Maggie giggled; the boots were wonderful. They emphasised her slim legs and she could only walk by swaying her hips.

Dressed in her play-clothes, Maggie pouted and touched up her mascara and rich red lipstick. Her reflection offered the promise of pure sex. With her eyes still firmly fixed on the wanton image in the mirror she slipped her hand down between her thighs and stroked the moist folds of her sex; she was getting wetter with every passing second. She glanced at her watch, wondering if there was time enough to bring this to its natural conclusion. Meanwhile busy fingers worked over her pleasure bud and she moaned softly as the pressure increased low in her belly. The whore in the mirror copied her move for move, writhing and pressing forward, legs apart, revealing the deep pink of her sex beneath the hem of the skirt. Maggie watched herself, watched her nipples harden within the shiny black top.

Then without warning she gasped for breath as an orgasm overtook her, making her convulse with delight and cry out with pure pleasure, and then she was still, slumped against the basins, trembling with sweet aftershocks.

It was nearly six, time to go and find Guido. Maggie glanced down at the boots and then slipped them off and put on the shoes she'd been wearing for work. At least this way she could hide the rest of her outfit under her coat.

Out in the corridor she hurried towards the fire exit.

'So there you are,' someone called, halting her in her tracks. 'I wondered where you'd got to.'

Maggie groaned inwardly. This was not happening to her. How had Simon Faraday tracked her down this time? He must have her on radar.

As if he was reading her mind, he said, 'I asked the guys on the front desk if you'd already gone home, and they told me you hadn't. What's this then,' he went on, admiring her make-up, 'out on a heavy date with your imaginary boyfriend?'

Up until now Maggie hadn't looked up; she knew exactly what she looked like and had no desire at all to see Simon's lecherous expression.

Simon caught hold of her arm. 'What's the matter?' he demanded. 'A little too near the mark, am I?' He pulled her towards him with a degree of unexpected aggression and her coat fell open.

Simon gasped, his eyes drinking in her mouth-watering appearance. 'What the…?' he began and stepping closer, tipped her face up to his and drooled at the breathtaking look of her.

'Well, well, well, what's going on here?' he said.

Maggie was speechless; what on earth could she say?

Simon grabbed her arms and pulled her closer.

'Well?' he demanded. 'Does your new man like you to dress up like a slut? Is that where you're going now? Maybe you like it a little rough, eh? Maybe our little bit of fun in the shower was just the thing that gets you off? Was it? Tell me, because trust me, I can play that game any time if that's what you want.'

Breathing heavily he pressed her back against the wall, forced his fingers between her thighs and with the other hand he molested her breasts.

'Stop it,' she warned, wriggling away from him, her mind racing. 'Don't you dare touch me. I have some say in this, you know. What I do is my business, not yours. As it is you've got it all wrong. I'm off to do a piece on a fetish club, and I can hardly go dressed in a flowery skirt and blouse, can I? This just arrived and I wanted to try it on, that's all.'

The lie sounded barely plausible, even to her. For a moment Simon froze and his eyes darkened; it seemed she'd hit a raw nerve, but she wasn't sure how or why.

'Are those the kinds of games you like to play then, Maggie?' he challenged. 'Fetish clubs, and things like that.'

'I'm not playing any games,' she snapped. She'd really had enough of obnoxious Simon. 'I've already told you, it's research. Now get out of my way. I'm meeting someone and I don't want to be late.' And remarkably, for once, he did as he was told.

Maggie made her way briskly towards the fire exit, and at no point did she look back to see Simon watching her go, his expression indicating the thoughts forming in his head.

Guido was waiting for Maggie in the car park, and touched his cap as he opened the rear car door, looking at her inquisitively.

'You okay?' he asked, taking her bag as she slipped off her shoes and pulled on the boots.

She nodded, a little bemused that Guido of all people should sound so concerned about her well-being. Looking back at the office block she saw Simon in a window watching the car draw away, and couldn't help wondering just what he was thinking, and perhaps more to the point, what it was he thought he'd discovered.

Chapter Ten

Once well out of town Guido pulled over into a quiet lay-by, got out of the car and opened the rear door.

Maggie looked out at him in surprise. 'What are we stopping for?' she asked.

'You forget the rules so quickly, don't you, Maggie?' he said. 'You're the slave here, remember? You do as you're told, you don't ask questions. Open your coat and get in the front.'

Maggie did as she was told, and Guido pulled a black leather blindfold out of his pocket and slipped it around Maggie's head, snugly over her eyes.

'There, now isn't that better?' he murmured. 'All wrapped up and ready to go. Max's pretty little toy.' He ran a hand over her face and then down to cup her breast, fingers teasing a nipple through the PVC and squeezing it hard until she gasped with pain. With his free hand he pulled the seatbelt across and buckled her in tight.

'You look a real treat, Maggie,' he said, pulling her hands together in her lap and cuffing her. 'Comfortable, are we?'

Maggie winced at the loss of freedom. 'No, of course

not,' she said. 'Why are you doing this, Guido? There's no need; you know I'll do whatever Max tells me.'

'Come, come, you must understand that sometimes obeying isn't enough, Maggie. You have to realise that in our world obedience implies you have a free will, that you can choose – where as in fact, Maggie, you can be used, abused, discarded on a whim. The mistake you make is in thinking you have any choice or any power.'

He squeezed a hand between her thighs. 'You don't need to know why you're being bound, just that you are and if you make too much noise or ask too many questions, I'll gag you as well.'

Maggie took a deep breath, trying to settle herself; it didn't do to let her imagination run amok. Guido's hand squeezed towards her sex, and she shuddered as a finger grazed across her sex lips.

'Mmmm, you feel so good.' The finger parted the moist flesh, and Maggie's instinctive reaction was to try and close her knees against him.

'I wouldn't try to resist if I were you,' he threatened menacingly. 'That would be unwise.

'Mmm, you're so tight and so wet, you dirty little bitch,' he went on as her thighs relaxed a little and gave him freer access to her. 'You're lucky Max is waiting for us, or I'd fuck you here and now,' he stated confidently, pressing kisses to her face and throat. 'Maybe I'll fuck you on the back, when he's done with you. What do you think?'

She shook her head, afraid to answer, and from behind the mask she felt him move away, felt his fingers leave her body, then the engine hummed into life and they pulled away.

It was a longer journey than she'd expected, but eventually the car drew to a halt, one of the doors opened, and Maggie immediately heard Max's voice.

'Good evening, Guido,' he said. 'Any problems?'

'None at all, sir,' the driver reported.

'Excellent. I've parked the other car over by the trees.'

Maggie heard some keys exchanging hands and then was aware of Max swapping places with Guido. 'Good evening, Maggie,' he said in a low tone.

She turned unseeing towards him. 'Good evening, master.'

Maggie felt him moving closer, felt his breath on her throat, felt him taking in the details of her appearance. She shivered, aware that every part of her, body and soul, longed for his approval and that in that moment she was totally his.

'You look magnificent, Maggie,' he said, stroking her arm.

'Master, please can you tell me where we're going?' she ventured.

He stroked her cheek and very gently kissed her lips. 'Maggie, you know better than that. You will learn only to speak when spoken to.' He stroked a finger across her lips, and then pushed something firm and hard between them into her mouth.

'Open wider,' he commanded, and Maggie didn't dare do otherwise. 'Did you talk to Guido on the way here?' he asked, and she shook her head.

'Do you know what this is, Maggie?'

She shook her head again.

'It's a leather gag, and unless you learn to be quiet I will make you wear it all weekend. Do you understand?'

Maggie nodded, struggling to swallow.

'Good. Just one more thing.'

She felt the soft leather collar slip around her throat, marking her as his property, although oddly enough far from being intimidated, it gave her a strange sense of comfort.

'There,' said Max, then turned the key in the ignition and the car slowly drew away.

Showered and comfortable in a white towelling robe, her tarty clothing discarded on the floor of the pretty cottage's bathroom, Maggie brushed her hair in the mirror, feeling happy and relaxed.

She went downstairs, where Max sat waiting for her in the quaint lounge, the table set with linen and crystal, champagne chilling in an ice bucket, Guido dressed in livery waiting to serve them.

She looked at Max, aware of how vulnerable she must look.

He smiled at her and extended a hand. 'Come over here, Maggie,' he beckoned. She did as she was told and stood in front of him. He slid a hand up her thigh, beneath the towelling. 'Undo your robe,' he ordered, and she did without a second's hesitation. 'Now take it off.'

Again she obeyed, aware of her nakedness, but aware that above everything else that doing as she was ordered pleased Max. Was this the true nature of slavery?

'Bend over the table,' he instructed, 'and spread your legs.'

Slowly she did, settling herself on the crisp linen, amongst the fine crockery, and even before Max touched her she felt a great wave of desire roll over her. She wanted him, and whatever that wanting brought.

Max ran his hands over her naked back, slid them between her legs, adjusting her position slightly so she was easier to explore. Maggie knew she was wet; she knew she was ready.

Max stepped back to admire his possession. Spread out on the table she looked an absolute feast. He beckoned to Guido, who handed him the crop. He didn't need a reason to punish her. He would punish her because he could. He would punish her because she wanted to.

Maggie was trembling as she waited for whatever was to follow. She didn't look round, but waited patiently. At last she was learning. He studied her, eyes moving appreciatively over the ripe curves of her buttocks, the wetness of her sex, engorged with pure desire. He knew Maggie was expecting him to fuck her – but first there was the matter of a punishment to dispense.

Max drew the crop back and relished the gasp of shock and horror as it found its mark across her bottom. On the table she convulsed as the pain coursed through her, her fists clenching on the fine white linen of the tablecloth.

'One,' she gasped after a few seconds.

'Very good, my dear,' said Max. 'I thought for a moment that you had forgotten the most basic of rules.'

The crop cracked down across the tops of her thighs. 'Two!' she sobbed.

Three and four were slightly less painful, striping the fleshy orbs of her backside. Her skin flushed scarlet under his attentions. Five and six were lower again, making her squeal as they caught the tender flesh. He could hear the tears in her voice as she called out the number of strokes.

He ran a hand over her glowing skin. 'Good girl... only another nine to go.' He felt her shudder as the realisation that there was much more to come hit home, and with it came stroke seven. This time Maggie screamed, giving in to the acute pain.

Eight. Nine. Ten; knowing the end was some distance away, lost deep in the pain. The crop rose and fell, each stroke counted out after the gasp or whimper or shriek in response to the hurt.

'All done,' he announced, having delivered number fifteen with added intensity. He placed the crop beside her on the table, where she could see the implement that had caused her so much discomfort and humiliation. His hands kneaded her raw and angry welts, and Maggie instinctively lifted her hips to absorb his touch. She was grateful for his punishment and even more so for the rewards it brought. Max smiled thinly and without any prelude unzipped his trousers and sank his throbbing cock deep into her cunt.

Maggie gasped and pressed back to encourage him deeper still. Max sighed appreciatively; she was as wet and hot as he had ever known her.

He slid a hand under her belly to seek out her clit, and then pulled her hand down to join his. Maggie writhed as his fingers found the engorged ridge, meeting him stroke for stroke, their bodies working in sexual harmony.

Max felt his orgasm building, coming closer and closer. He felt her sex pulsate around his cock, felt her shiver and writhe beneath him. He grabbed her hair and pulled her up off the table. She cried out his name, her back arching as he clenched his jaw, stabbed with his groin, pinning her hips to the table, and filled her with his seed.

Her sobs of pleasure filled the room, and then she slumped forward again as if fainting.

Chapter Eleven

Maggie woke the following morning, safe in her bedroom back at Max's elegant townhouse; her body marked by the crop, her mind indelibly marked by

Max's power over her.

She showered and made her way downstairs, naked except for her collar, for that was all that had been left out for her on the dresser.

Mrs Griffin served breakfast in the dining room overlooking the park, and Max invited her to join him at the table and not, as she suspected he might, on her knees at his feet.

'I'm very pleased with your progress, my dear,' he said, as they sat in the sitting room a little later, drinking coffee and relaxing in each other's company. 'You've come a long way in a remarkably short time, Maggie.'

She smiled at him, basking in his approval. Her body was at his disposable. Her marks were his marks. He sat on the sofa with her legs over his lap, reading the morning newspaper and stroking her thighs, as one might a much-loved cat.

'Your basic training will very soon be coming to an end,' he said casually, not lifting his attention or his gaze from the paper.

Maggie stiffened and felt the colour drain from her face, the sense of well-being evaporating instantly. Surely he couldn't mean what she thought he meant; it was too soon. Max looked at her, his features softening as if he could read her mind.

'My dear Maggie, I explained to you when we first met that my role as a training master is to help find the submissive, the slave within you,' he said. 'I bring it to the fore and then find the way to harness it sexually and emotionally, and I truly believe in your case that has already been accomplished. Look at you, look how far you've come. Am I not right?'

Maggie nodded, although at the same time she could feel her eyes filling with tears. This was not what she expected at all.

'Another couple of weeks and you will be ready to be sold to a permanent master,' he went on. 'A master who will train you as he wants, to his way of doing things. Trust me, my dear, the longer you stay with me the harder it will be for you to make that transition. I have shown you what is possible, what is in your heart, the nature of submission and obedience and the most basic rules, now you need to apply all you have learnt to a more permanent arrangement.' He sipped his coffee, eyes moving very slowly up over her body. 'Some girls take months to get to this point, but you're a fast leaner, a natural, but I knew that the day I first saw you. It is very nearly time for you to move on.'

Maggie knew that what sounded like a compliment was in fact the hastening of the end of their arrangement. She felt an ache in her chest and struggled to hold back the tears. How could she possibly bear to lose what she had only so recently found? 'I... I don't want to go,' she whispered.

Max smiled, stroking her thigh. 'There is no need to worry, you won't just be sold to any old undesirable, I can assure you of that. Our slave auctions are by invitation only, and those who attend are already part of an inner circle of connoisseurs. It's a unique club of carefully chosen members. The auction will take place over a weekend at one of my fellow member's country estate. It will be fine, trust me.'

She looked at him anxiously, and Max leant close and very gently stroked the hair back off her brow. 'Don't look so worried, we have time enough yet, my little one. And you knew this would happen sooner or later.'

Maggie nodded. 'But I thought it wouldn't be for a long time yet,' she began, aware of how vulnerable and needy she sounded. How could she explain to Max that she believed, hoped that their journey together had only just begun, that in some way even though he was her master he was also her guide into a foreign world.

'I have learnt to follow my instinct in these things,' he said. 'But enough of this, tonight I have arranged for us to go to the theatre.'

The theatre? She looked at him in surprise. There were so many things she wanted to ask him, so many things she wanted to say, how on earth could he possibly think of such a thing now?

Max's smile broadened. 'It will be your first formal introduction to some of the most influential members of our club, Maggie. These social events are very important to us – and I know you will not let me down.'

Maggie nodded, trying hard to hide her anxieties.

'Smile,' he said. 'It will be all right. Besides, surely you must know by now that I will always be here for you.'

She stared at him in astonishment, for it was by far the most intimate thing he had ever said to her, but any sense of comfort was short-lived. 'I'm always here for my slaves, Maggie, that is part of my role,' he continued. 'You are the latest in a long line of slaves, but trust me; very few come back for my help. Your fears will pass.

'Now, I have business in town this afternoon, so while I'm away I suggest you rest. It's going to be a long night. When you've rested Mrs Griffin will wake you and help you get ready for your night out.'

'So, all ready to meet the rest of the club, are you?'

Maggie started from her doze to find Guido leaning over the bed. As she tried to move he pinned her arms down and held her tight. Maggie looked round, trying to shake the sleep from her brain and at the same time work out exactly what was going on. The bedroom curtains were drawn but outside it was still daylight, and she sensed she hadn't been asleep for long.

'I'll scream,' she warned, trying to prise him off her.

Guido laughed. 'Really? And what good do you think that would do? Haven't I already told you that as a slave you're always available for whoever wants to use you for whatever purpose? And besides,' he grinned, eyes alight with mischief, 'your master has gone to pick something up from town, or maybe he's gone to pick up someone. And Mrs Griffin? Well, she's down in the basement doing I don't know what, but trust me, whatever it is she isn't going to hear anything from up here, and that includes you screaming like a spoiled brat.'

'What are you doing here?' Maggie demanded, trying to gain some initiative from him. 'Why aren't you driving Max?'

He shrugged. 'Max doesn't want me with him all the time.' He moved her wrists and held them above her head with one hand, while with the other he pulled down the duvet. She was naked except for her collar.

'Very nice,' he leered, eyeing her body hungrily. 'Now, are you going to do as I tell you or are you going to try my patience?'

Maggie strained against his grip but he held her fast.

Guido's expression hardened. 'Another thing you should bear in mind,' he went on unmoved, 'is that you don't fool me for a second. I know you enjoy being treated like this. I see in you what Max sees: a natural submissive, someone who likes to be dominated, to be vulnerable in the control of others. You might struggle but we both know that you like what's on offer. And when you're up for auction? Word gets around about who is worth bidding for. I don't know what Max told you, but there are some real bastards in that club of his.

It wouldn't do for me to put a word in with them about you, now would it?'

Maggie looked up at him. 'You're a bastard too, Guido,' she stated defiantly.

He nodded. 'Oh yes, you could be right. But Max and I both, don't forget that. Don't be fooled by him, Maggie. Max and I are two faces of the same animal.'

She shivered, wondering if it was true, and before she could react Guido pulled a loop of rope from his jacket pocket and slipped it over both her wrists, jerking it tight, wrapping it round and round on itself until she was secured. Not that she resisted him any more; there was little point. Guido's power, like Max's, extended beyond the physical.

Once her arms were tied to the bed-head Guido took his time looking her over again. 'Open your legs,' he ordered. 'We won't do anything too rough for now, after all, Max's friends will have the use of you tonight, so we can't have you too sore, now can we?' As he spoke he secured each ankle to the corners of the bed, opening her legs wide, then pushing a pillow under her hips he stood back to admire his handiwork.

Open, tied down, totally humiliated and ready for him, Maggie closed her eyes; she wasn't even safe asleep in her bed.

'It's such a shame you won't be here too much longer,' he said. 'Just when I was developing a taste for you.' And then Guido shocked her by crouching and lapping at her sex, burying his face tight between her thighs, working his tongue and nose into her, drinking her in. Maggie gasped and tried to wriggle away from him, but where was there to go? Her wrists dragged on the rope as Guido pulled her onto his tongue, stiff to enter her like a tiny wet penis.

His eyes alight with lust he looked up at her from

between her parted thighs, his tongue delving inside her. 'Does Max ever tell you how good you taste?' he mumbled, withdrawing his mouth for a moment. 'How good you smell?' He breathed deep, savouring her fragrance.

Maggie closed her eyes as Guido's fingers joined his tongue, fingers that not only breached her sex but also breached her anus, exploring the most secret parts of her body. He began to slide them in and out, stretching, making her writhe at the intense sensations despite her shame.

'Oh yes, Maggie, I'm going to miss you,' Guido whispered into the soft flesh of her sex, the words dark and resonant, Maggie feeling them as much as hearing them. 'Mind you, knowing Max it won't be too long before he finds a lovely replacement for me to enjoy.'

Maggie shuddered, trying to block out the cruel words, and despite the feelings of shame the passion was beginning to stir, each movement of Guido's tongue and fingers fanning the flames. She cringed, knowing Guido was as aware of her body's response as she was. He mumbled encouragement as she began to move instinctively against his mouth, her sex flooding with traitorous juices of excitement.

Even though tied to the bed her body sought his caresses, lifting as high as the bonds would permit, then she heard Guido snigger hurtfully as he pulled away and she strained to find his tongue.

'You really are a little whore,' he snorted, wiping his chin with the back of his hand.

'I know,' she said, her voice thick with desire. 'Why don't you fuck me, Guido, please?'

'You think I wouldn't?' he said.

Maggie felt his cock pressing at the lips of her sex, felt him trying to find his way into her body, and she, without conscious thought, lifted her hips a fraction to ease his entry. She gasped, still shocked by the way her body demanded satisfaction and pleasure. He stabbed his pelvis forward and sank his cock into her, stretching and filling her. Maggie loved the moment of penetration, the sensation making her shiver with delight, and then she heard a moan of acceptance and knew it was hers.

Guido sat back from her, fingers working over her clit, his shaft moving slow and deep inside her pulsating cunt, relishing the sensation of her body closing around him, while his other hand nipped and pulled at her breasts and nipples. Maggie tried to hold back the growing wave of gratification, tried to fight the heat building between her thighs, but knew it was a pointless exercise, merely delaying the inevitable.

Guido was driving them both relentlessly towards release. Maggie knew it wouldn't be long before both of them reached the point of no return. Above her he threw back his head, forcing himself deep, deep into her, his face contorted with the effort of struggling to withhold his climax, and just when she thought Guido was losing control she felt the waves of orgasm break over her, felt her sex sucking her tormentor dry.

Guido collapsed onto her, gasping for breath, sweat dripping from his face onto the pillow.

'Maybe I should leave you tied up,' he rambled. 'Maybe I should let Mrs Griffin find you like this. Maybe you'd like that... and maybe she would too.'

'No, please,' she whispered wearily, 'please just untie me.'

Guido pinched her nipple. 'So you know about Mrs Griffin then?'

Maggie was confused, just wanting to be left alone now. 'What about Mrs Griffin?'

'Didn't you know she was Max's first ever slave?' he goaded her, grinning broadly. 'I've seen the photographs of when he was training her. He had her pierced here... and here... to mark her as his.' He stroked Maggie's nipples to demonstrate, and then her clit. 'He was younger then, of course, so he thought it better if she went to an older master who could continue her training appropriately. And then a couple of years ago when her master died she came home to her roots. And I just know she'd be delighted to find you all nicely tied up for her. She likes women as much as men; I know that for a fact. Perhaps she likes them even more than she likes men. Would you like me to call her up, so she can demonstrate?'

Maggie pulled on the ropes that held her wrists. 'No, please Guido, please untie me.'

'Why should I?'

Maggie froze. What reason was there? What was there that she could offer him he hadn't already had or could take? Under Max's roof she was a slave, there for the benefit of others. Not Guido's slave, true, but a slave nonetheless, a thing to be used and fucked on the whim of masters and mistresses. And he was right; if Mrs Griffin came in now she was as likely to fuck her as anyone else.

Guido pulled out of her, his flaccid cock wet against her inner thigh. 'Don't worry, Maggie, I won't leave you tied up. We can't have Max's pride and joy getting cramp or rope burns on those pretty wrists or ankles. At least not tonight, not when you're going to be on show.'

With relief she lay back and let Guido untie her, longing for him to leave so she could curl up into a ball and go back to sleep and pretend his visit was no more than a bad dream.

Behind the false mirror Max watched avidly. He didn't like to admit it, even to himself, but seeing Guido fucking Maggie had ignited a little flicker of jealously in his gut. He shook his head. Maybe the sooner she went the better.

In the small bedroom Maggie whimpered as Guido ran his hands over her naked flesh, his exploration demeaning and perfunctory, a parting gesture. Maggie tried to turn away but Guido caught her hair. 'Aren't slaves supposed to do something else?' he asked darkly, jerking her head up towards him.

Maggie stared at him, apparently uncomprehending, so Guido knelt on the side of the bed and ran his limp cock over her cheek, leaving a trail of moisture in its wake. Comprehension dawned on her face, then Guido jerked her head and she drew his cock into her mouth as Max had taught her to do.

'That's better,' Guido sighed as she licked his cock and balls, then he pulled away and let go of her. 'Sweet dreams,' he said, and then left the room.

Guido was close to the end of his training too, and Max would be glad to see the back of him.

It was several hours later that Max watched Maggie walking downstairs towards him in the evening dress he had chosen for her. Boned and cut in a soft velvet, the colour of red wine, it complemented her creamy complexion and emphasised her narrow waist and full hips, the skirt falling like heavy curtain to the floor. She looked almost regal, not a glimmer of the encounter with Guido showing on her face or in her demeanour.

Mrs Griffin had helped her with her make-up, and to dress her hair into a soft bun with tendrils that fell around her face to soften her features. Standing at the bottom of the stairs, caught in the lamplight, she looked exquisite, a possession truly worthy of a man of his status.

Her eyes glittered with delight; she knew she looked good. Max nodded his approval and indicated that she should turn around so he could assess her fully.

'Very nice, but I have a few final touches to add before we leave, my dear,' he said, and produced a small jewellery box from the pocket of his dinner jacket. Inside was a fine black ribbon with a tiny M picked out in diamonds, and matching drop earrings.

'There we are, your dress collar,' he said, as she turned to let him fasten it around her slender throat.

Beneath the dress Max knew she was totally naked, because he had watched her being prepared for him in the false mirror. Watching Mrs Griffin neatly trim her sex, watching Maggie submit to the woman's ministrations, delighted him in ways he could not explain and was the perfect antidote to witnessing her with Guido.

Mrs Griffin knew all about the mirror and had carefully guided her charge to stand in front of it so that when she massaged Maggie's back and breasts with perfumed oils it was as much for Max's benefit as for Maggie's.

Opening the girl's thighs to trim her pubic curls, drawing kohl around her eyes and rich red lipstick around her full lips had all been done with an eye on their unseen audience too, and Max appreciated every second.

As Maggie turned towards him now, eyes demurely downcast he felt a great wave of pride and affection toward her. By now he knew every inch of her body and her mind. For an instant he felt a tinge of regret that she would be leaving so soon, but his instinct told him it was time to move on before she became too attached or perhaps, he thought, worse still, before he did.

'Very good,' he said. 'Now lift up your skirt, there is something else I have for you.'

Maggie blushed and then looked up at him.

Max met her eyes. 'You have something to say, little one?' he pressed, but Maggie shook her head, knowing better than to question his instructions, whatever her thoughts, and did as she was ordered, pulling her skirt up above her waist.

Max nodded and admired what was on show. High-heeled shoes emphasised her shapely legs, and above smooth thighs the ridge of her pubis was oiled and soft and smooth as a silk.

Max took a second box from another pocket, and inside were two lengths of silver chain, fixed together in the middle of one so that they formed a T shape. The length of the T wrapped tight around Maggie's waist, while the other pulled up between her legs, fixed at the front of her belly by a small padlock, with Max's initials embossed on it.

The chain sat snugly between the lips of her sex and between the cheeks of her bottom, fastened to press tight into her flesh.

Max smiled as he tested the tautness by slipping his fingers under the links. It looked exquisite nestled deep in her sex, and he knew it would rub and nip at the delicate flesh every time she moved so that all evening there wouldn't be a moment when she wasn't aware of her subjugation and slavery. He stroked down to the rise of her mons, pressing the chain onto the ridge of her clit. The silver links rubbing gently against her would also make her very wet.

He scrutinised her closely. 'Comfortable?' he asked, and she nodded nervously. 'Good, then drop your skirt back into place; it's time to leave.'

Mrs Griffin picked up a black velvet cape from the hall stand, the lining chosen to match Maggie's dress exactly, and wrapped it around the girl's shoulders. With the hood up she looked enigmatic and mysterious and Max was struck – as he often had been over the years – of the delightful paradox of having a girl as both slave and companion who to the eyes of the world was beautiful and demure, and yet knowing that beneath the sophisticated exterior lurked a slave who would do anything he commanded, whose body and soul were his to possess, to take or to give away as he chose. It was heady stuff.

Maggie settled in the back of the car as they made their way across town, the chain nipping her sex like eager fingers. Max started up a conversation and Guido watched her every move in the rear-view mirror. What would her life be like after the auction? It seemed so cruel to be sold when she had only just acclimatised to Max's way of life.

The light was beginning to fade as they drew up outside the theatre. Guido got out to open the car door for them, touching his cap in a gesture of respect and subservience that Maggie suspected was little more than an act. He caught her eye and winked, and she coloured as Max glanced at her.

'He is nothing,' he stated as they walked to the theatre entrance. 'He may use your body occasionally, but you must understand that's all it is. He has no power over you that you do not give him.'

Maggie stared at him in amazement. 'You know about Guido?' she gasped.

Max nodded. 'Of course I do,' he said. 'I know about everything that does on under my roof. Besides, he is still one of my pupils, just as you are.'

The idea horrified Maggie. 'So will he be a master one day too?' she asked.

Max shrugged. 'Who can say? While Guido is in my service he will receive the training, he will go through the motions, but my experience is that masters are born, not made. I'm not sure he has the right balance of care and control.'

As he finished speaking a man in a dinner suit approached them and smiled. 'Good evening, Mr Jordan,' he said politely, 'how very nice to see you again. Your box is ready.'

'And my friends?' Max asked.

'Most are already seated,' the man informed him.

Maggie looked at the man curiously. Did everyone know about Max, or was this man another member of the club? An usher showed them upstairs to a luxury box where two other men and two women were already waiting for the performance to begin. Maggie didn't need to be told that the women were slaves; their whole demeanour gave them away. Like her they were beautifully dressed in evening gowns, and both had little black ribbons around their throats and sat in silence with eyes downcast.

She shivered, aware that she was glimpsing again the magical doorway into another world. Max indicated that she should sit alongside him, so she did so and sat with her gaze fixed on the floor like her fellow slaves. Max nodded greetings to his fellow theatregoers, and then the orchestra began the overture, making the prospect of any conversation unlikely.

The musical was a lavish production of Hamlet, with a full orchestra adding to the already rich story. As the tragedy began to unfold Maggie looked around at the other people in the box. Both men where in their late forties or early fifties, distinguished and worldly. One of the females was around Maggie's age, whilst the other, a tiny blonde with big blue eyes, looked younger and was quite obviously overawed by their surroundings.

Her master rested a hand on her thigh, and slowly but surely lifted her dress so he could stroke her exposed cunt.

In the boxes opposite Maggie saw that other members of the audience appeared to be slaves and masters too, each of the women wearing the same black band around their throats. Were all these people a part of Max's exclusive club?

In the box alongside theirs was a woman Maggie recognised, dressed in black velvet. It was Freya, and beside her was Beau, wearing a black tie that performed much the same function as the chokers the female slaves wore.

During the interval Max and Maggie made their way to a luxurious anteroom on the same floor, where uniformed staff served champagne cocktails to the twenty or so masters and mistresses and their charges. It appeared that only the masters engaged in conversation with each other.

'So, is this your latest?' said a large man sipping champagne from a glass dwarfed by his huge hand. On his arm was a diminutive brunette, who stood no taller than his chest.

Max nodded. 'Indeed it is, Cedric,' he said.

'And is this the girl you'll be putting up for auction?'

'Yes, but have no fear, you'll get a chance to put her through her paces before the sale.'

The tall man laughed. 'I was sorry to have missed your last house party. I hear Mike's new filly is quite a find, too.'

Max nodded in acknowledgement. 'Indeed she is,' he confirmed, and Maggie blushed as she realised they were talking about the night she had helped Max with Kay. She glanced around the room from the corner of her eye, trying to pick out familiar faces, trying to see if her lodger and her master were there too.

'There will always be another time, Cedric,' Max added.

'Yes, but not necessarily with this one,' he looked her up and down. 'What did you say her name was?'

'Maggie.'

'Maggie...' The tall man tried the name out on his tongue, as if tasting some unusual food. 'How about tonight?' he then suggested. 'I will lend you Bella, if you like. I know you've always had a soft spot for her.'

Max's expression didn't falter. 'Later perhaps,' he declined the offer tactfully. 'We've hardly time during the interval.'

'I suppose not,' the man conceded. 'But I'd like a look at what's on offer.'

Max clapped Cedric on the shoulder. 'You are always so eager, my dear chap,' he chuckled. 'There will be plenty of time before the auction. Now come along and have another glass of champagne.'

Beside him the little brunette's eyes darkened, and Maggie could almost taste her jealousy.

Max guided Maggie towards one of the waiters, but Cedric waved him away. 'Not for me at the moment, I'll catch up with you later,' he said.

Max snorted. 'The man is a pig,' he murmured under his breath. 'He and Bella have been together since she was sixteen. In essence she is his slave and he is her master, but it's well known that she rules his little harem with a rod of iron. If she doesn't like the slave he buys then life as one of Cedric's stable can be a trial by fire. He should sell her; it would do her the world of good to feel the taste of the crop wielded with some purpose.'

Maggie shivered and turned to look at the couple's retreating backs. It hadn't occurred to her that the usual jealousies and insecurities had any place in this strange world. What if Cedric decided to buy her? What would life be like then?

The five-minute bell rang and everyone made their way back to the auditorium, where Maggie again looked around at the faces of the audience as they settled back into their seats. As the lights went down, across the heads of them Cedric smiled and lifted a hand in her direction, and quickly Maggie looked away, not wanting to encourage him. As he caught the gesture Max's hand dropped onto her thigh possessively.

'Don't worry,' he whispered. 'I won't let Cedric have you.'

Maggie shivered, wondering what influence Max had to ensure Cedric was kept at bay, and as the curtain went up for the second half she couldn't help worrying about what the rest of the evening might hold for her.

As the final curtain call was taken and the applause gradually died away Max rose effortlessly. 'Now for dinner, my dear,' he said to her. 'I don't know about you, but I'm absolutely ravenous.'

She had assumed they would be taken on somewhere by Guido; a private house or a restaurant, perhaps, but in fact a uniformed usher directed them back to the anteroom where double doors had been opened onto a luxurious dining room set with candles and linen and cut crystal that glittered magically in the flickering light.

Tables had been set around the room, the centre dominated by a larger table on a raised dais. It was here that Max, Maggie and the two couples who'd shared their box were led. Maggie blushed, feeling uncomfortable as the focus of attention, for all the other diners had taken their seats before she and Max were shown to theirs.

The food was exquisite, the service immaculate, but all the time they were eating, above the buzz of conversation and laughter, Maggie could sense the electricity of expectation in the air. As coffee was served one of the waiters went from table to table with an ice bucket, and each master drew a folded piece of paper from inside. Maggie noticed that when they reached the top table, while the other masters took a piece of paper Max politely declined and the waiter moved on.

Eventually, once all the tables were clear except for coffee cups and liqueur glasses, Max turned to her. 'Maggie,' he said.

She looked at him anxiously. 'Yes, master?' she whispered.

'Get up and take off your dress.'

She cringed inwardly, and for a few seconds stared at him in dismay and horror. Surely he couldn't possibly mean it? Of all the things she'd been expecting this wasn't one of them. There had to be at least forty people gathered in the dining room, not counting the waiting staff. She bit her lip, feeling her colour rise.

Max's expression hardened. 'Well, Maggie?' he pressed. 'Would you prefer that I rip it off you and whip your disobedient little arse until you scream for mercy?'

Slowly, her pulse roaring in her ears, she rose and the hubbub of conversation dropped to a low murmur, and then fell silent completely.

Slowly she reached back and unfastened the zip of the evening gown, feeling the heat of humiliation and embarrassment coursed through her veins as she caught Cedric's eyes. His ruddy face was full of undisguised lust. Slowly she slipped the straps down off one shoulder and then the next, and slid the dress down to reveal her full breasts. Her hands were trembling and it took every shred of courage and self-control not to pull the fabric back up and cover herself.

The dress lowered to her waist and she eased it down over her hips to reveal the chain around her waist and between her legs. There was an appreciative murmur as the dress finally dropped to the floor, and she looked at Max, her complexion flushed crimson.

He took her hand. 'Get on the table,' he commanded.

Maggie let out a tiny whimper, audible only to those around them. Even so, she did as she was told and lay down on her back amongst the remaining silverware and crockery.

'Very good,' he said. 'Now open your legs wide and touch yourself.'

Maggie froze for a moment, but his eyes were broody and she knew there was no going back. 'Stroke yourself, my little one,' he ordered. 'Don't let me down, now.'

Maggie closed her eyes against the shame engulfing her, and sliding a finger beneath the chain began to circle her clitoris. Her sex was embarrassingly wet, her clit already sensitised by the constant rubbing of the chain links.

'Give my friends a little more,' he urge, and with her other hand Maggie began to stroke her breasts, teasing her nipples into rigid peaks. She could feel the eyes of the all people in the room upon her, terrified and mortified and yet in the same instant breathlessly excited by the feeling it ignited in her, the sense of power rippling though her. She began to finger herself more urgently, her thumb working her pleasure bud, and she started moving against the caress, lifting her hips, opening her legs wider still. And against all the odds she felt the pleasure begin to build in the pit of her belly.

'Ask me,' Max reminded her, drawing her out of the dreamy state into which she was falling.

Ask him, her mind urged; ask him now before it's too late. 'Please, master,' she murmured, 'may I come?'

He chuckled approvingly. 'Yes, little one,' he said, and eased a finger deep into her sex. She cried out in pleasure, lifting herself to give him greater access. As she did the first wave of orgasm rolled through her body, and she could feel her sex closing around him and surrendered.

She fucked his fingers like a whore, driving herself on and on to greater and greater heights until finally she could take no more and fell back, all tension gone, lying still, aware again of the eyes on her and the press of the table against her back.

Max stood and stepped away, took an envelope from his pocket and opened it.

Maggie closed her eyes again, unable to imagine what might follow. 'Number seventeen,' he announced to the room, and Maggie stiffened; what did that mean?

There was a general murmur amongst the diners, and then a guffaw of delight from someone on the far side of the room, and then Maggie realised with repulsion that not only was she the cabaret, she was also first prize in the raffle!

With her eyes still closed in a futile attempt to block out what was happening to her, Max handed an unseen master the key to the padlock and cold hands slipped under the chain to unfasten her. 'You're so wet,' drooled a gruff voice. 'Your cunt looks so succulent... good enough to eat...'

Maggie was almost afraid to open her eyes, but she had to, and was confronted by a craggy, elderly man looming over her. Not that his age or appearance mattered, of course; she had no say in the matter; he'd won her and that was his only concern.

'Get up on all fours,' he ordered, and Maggie did as she was told and felt the man struggle up onto the table behind her, heard him unfasten his fly, and felt him push her head down onto the tabletop so that her bottom and sex where presented for him.

'That's better,' he wheezed, his fingers pushing deep inside her, and then she was aware of his cock nuzzling and demanding entry at the engorged entrance of her sex, and of a murmur of approval rippling through the onlookers as he eased his cock into her vulnerable body.

Grunting like an animal he stabbed with his hips and embedded his erection fully inside Maggie, one hand on her hip, the other seeking her swaying breasts to roll and pinch her throbbing nipples. Maggie whimpered against the discomfort, so very shamefully close to an orgasm. Behind her the old man pushed more aggressively and she guessed it wouldn't take much to draw him over the edge. Then just as she began to find his rhythm, accepting her fate and wanting to conclude it promptly, the man slapped her buttocks sharply with a rigid leather paddle. She bucked instinctively and he snorted with delight.

'Ride me, you lovely little bitch!' he guffawed triumphantly, like a jockey driving his mount on to greater efforts. He beat her again, harder this time, and it was obvious to Maggie that her pain excited him. She cried out as he struck a third time, the slaps in time with his ever-quickening thrusts, and then they were both there at the pinnacle and Maggie felt him come, felt his cock throbbing deep, deep inside her, and cried out as the waves of pleasure swamped over her.

Chapter Twelve

'Maggie?'

She looked up from her desk, her mind a million miles away from the bustling offices of the magazine. It was the first day in almost two weeks that Maggie had been back in to work, preferring the peace and quiet and thinking space of working from home. Her prolonged absence meant that there were a huge pile of notes and post in the in-tray for her to sort through, and innumerable messages on the answer machine. Not that Maggie was unduly worried, she had already emailed in the stories and articles she'd been working on, well inside the deadline, so the day had been spent mostly on administration and sorting out ideas for future features and articles with the editor.

Across the desk Simon grinned at her. 'Well, well, well, nice to see you back at long last, Maggie,' he said. 'So how did your research go the other week? Recovered, have you? I've been wondering where you've been hiding. I was going to give you a ring to see how you are. I have to say, your outfit – the one you had on when I last saw you? – it took me by complete surprise. I didn't have you down as the kind of girl who likes fetish gear. Mind you, we live and learn; they always say it's the quiet ones you've got to watch. And I must say,' his voice dropped to a conspiratorial whisper, 'you looked fucking gorgeous in that gear. I could have screwed you there and then.'

Maggie felt her hackles beginning to rise. This was getting ridiculous. 'Please go away, Simon,' she said bluntly. 'I'm really busy, and I don't want to talk to you.'

He blew a lurid kiss at her. 'Oh come on, baby,' he

went on, totally undeterred. 'You and I have got unfinished business together.'

Maggie sighed. 'I don't think so, Simon,' she disagreed. This was getting way beyond a joke, and as she spoke she surreptitiously turned the computer screen away from him and clicked the mouse so that the email she had just been reading disappeared behind other pages. It was the thing she feared most – the email from Max Jordan with details of the forthcoming slave auction. It seemed that every time she had any dealings with Max at work they coincided with running in to Simon.

'Look,' he said, his voice still lowered so no one else could hear their conversation. 'We just got off on the wrong foot, that's all. I'm very attracted to you; you must know that. I only want to know you better, that's all. Why not give it a chance, Mags? Let's start over, shall we? What have you got to lose? You looked bloody fantastic in that PVC outfit, and I'd have sold my soul to have taken you out that night.'

Deep down she was pleased to have made such an impression, it was just a shame that she had no other feelings for Simon other than immense dislike and pure annoyance. He was like a mosquito that kept buzzing around bugging her, but for the sake of good manners she made every effort to keep her expression and her tone as neutral as she could manage. 'Simon, I keep telling you I'm not interested,' she reiterated. 'But you just don't seem to get it, do you? So I'm going to lay it on the line one more time. I'm not interested in you, and I've already told you that I'm already seeing someone else, and if you persist in harassing me I'm going to make a complaint. Now is *that* clear enough for you?'

It wasn't quite all true, but she was hoping it would deter him from harassing her.

'Really?' Simon said sceptically, ignoring the threat. 'That's all very convenient. So tell me again, where did you find him? In a lonely-hearts ad? Or did a friend take pity on you and fix you up with some no hoper.'

It was all Maggie could do not to slap his smug face. 'That's it; I don't want to talk to you, Simon,' she said, reaching the end of her tether. 'I've got a few more things to do here and then?'

'And then you're off home to see your imaginary boyfriend?' he said with an infuriating grin, and then sauntered back off across the office.

Maggie looked away, not trusting herself to say anything. Things were bad enough already. Max's instructions to her were explicit. Guido was to pick her up from her house the following day, Friday, at lunchtime. She was to ensure to keep the whole weekend and Monday free. There would be an exhibition on the first evening, when the various lots up for sale would be put on view for the masters, mistresses, and any guests to examine, and then they would be put through their paces for anyone who requested it. On Saturday morning the viewing would continue and then after lunch the sale would begin in earnest.

Maggie stared at the computer screen, a great wave of grief and nervousness rising in her chest. She had come so far over the last few weeks since meeting Max, without him the journey undertaken would have been impossible. He had become such an important part of her life and she feared losing him almost more than she feared the unknown.

Maggie glanced up at the office clock; by this time tomorrow she would be well on her way to the mysterious location, just a lot in a slave auction, numbered, catalogued and ready to be sold to the highest bidder. She shivered and tried to still her panic by turning her attention back to the practicalities. The email said she was to wear a long coat, black stockings and her collar – nothing else. Guido would have the rest of her outfit when he collected her. If she was honest with herself, Simon Faraday and his unwanted attentions were the last of her worries.

'How on earth do I get into this?' she asked, looking at Guido, who had arrived promptly with a black cardboard box tied around with a huge red ribbon.

In her hand was a black rubber corset with attached suspenders, cut to support her breasts but not quite cover them, and it was open at the crotch to reveal her sex lips. Guido handed her a container of talcum powder.

'Dust plenty on yourself and in the corset, and then roll it up and pull it on,' he instructed her. 'When you're done I'll polish you.'

They were standing in the hallway of her house, with an overnight bag at her feet, and it occurred to Maggie that Guido fully expected her to dress in front of him. It was strange how things had changed. She slipped off her raincoat under his watchful gaze, praying he didn't want to fuck her before they left. Knowing that Max wanted her to make him proud she had carefully oiled her body and meticulously trimmed her pubic hair, just as Mrs Griffin would have prepared her had they been at his house. Make-up and perfume carefully applied, she was aware of the paradox of wanting to please Max and yet at the same time knowing that each passing minute drew her closer and closer to losing her place with him.

Guido watched with icy amusement as she wriggled into the tight rubber corset, helping her pull it up over her hips and ribs and then breasts, easing the straps up over her shoulders and then with a soft cloth and a little spray canister buffing the latex to high shine. Maggie looked at herself in the hall mirror, the stretchy material seemed to hold her in and push her out in all the right places, making her breasts appear full and ripe above a narrow waist and rounded hips.

Guido's hands moved appreciatively over her tightly encased frame, and stopped buffing long enough to slip a hand between her thighs. 'It suits you,' he said, dropping to his knees to help her fasten the suspenders to the tops of her stockings.

His close attention caused her to blush. 'Who is going to be at this auction, Guido?' she asked anxiously. 'Will Kay and Mike be there, and all those people from the theatre?'

He looked up at her. 'Probably, and a lot of the others besides,' he confirmed. 'And the old guard as well, members who only come out of the woodwork to take a long hard look at the new blood.'

'And where is this place we're going to?'

'My, my, but we really are nervous, aren't we?' he mocked. 'It's a place up north, a country estate owned by Sir Hugh. He and Max are old friends, they go back a long way. He's a good man, and if you're lucky maybe he'll buy you. Or maybe you could persuade Max to give you to him as an early Christmas present.'

Maggie felt her eyes filling up with tears. How could she possibly tell Guido that she had barely slept the night before worrying about what might happen to her, wondering where she might end up and with whom. She had no idea what the rules of the game were. Then to her total surprise Guido straightened up and put his arm around her. 'Don't worry,' he said comfortingly, pulling her close. 'It'll be all right.'

'I don't know if it will, Guido,' she said openly.

'Where's Max? Why isn't he here too?'

'He's gone on ahead to help with the arrangements. But really, you shouldn't get upset. This is the way it goes. Max will make sure it works out all right for Maggie. He's got a knack with this sort of thing. All his girls have ended up okay. Honestly, his slaves command a high price, and you're one of his all time favourites. You'll be just fine. Max will see to it.'

Maggie was grateful for his kindness, even if she suspected it would be short-lived. Guido looked at his watch. 'Come on, you better get your coat on, we've a way to go yet.'

He was right. The drive to Sir Hugh's country estate seemed to take hours. Maggie's skin felt hot and damp under the rubber corset and her coat. As cityscapes gave way to rolling countryside and lush green hills, she watched fascinated, lulled into a waking doze by the constant movement of the car as the miles unfolded. On one occasion as the car swung out to overtake a lorry Maggie, disturbed awake by the manoeuvre, shifted position and realised how hot and uncomfortable she was in the corset.

Guido smiled at her in the rear-view mirror. 'Why don't you take your coat off?' he suggested.

For once she agreed with him, and oblivious to what sort of image she presented in the back of the car she slipped it off, curled up on the backseat with the coat under her head and let sleep claim her.

Eventually the car slowed and Maggie opened her eyes just as they drew up to a huge pair of wrought-iron gates. Guido slowed to a crawl while a camera on the wall scanned them thoughtfully, its single critical eye watching them closely. Slowly, haltingly the gates creaked into life, and once moving swung open silently, allowing them to drive on to the estate.

The avenue that led to the house swept in through a copse of trees, finally opening out onto a dramatic vista – an old country house surrounded by a moat and acres of rolling parkland, with a herd of red deer grazing under some distant oaks. Maggie gasped. It was far, far grander than anything she had anticipated.

It was built on a great square. Outbuildings and walls with turrets and castellations led the eye to the main house where ornate formal gardens flanked each side of the main entrance, which was reached over a drawbridge.

'Impressive, huh?' said Guido, as they drove slowly along the sweeping avenue to the house.

It was quite an understatement.

'We're staying here?' gasped Maggie, dragging her coat on; there was no way she wanted to arrive wearing nothing but the exotic rubber corset.

'No, don't cover yourself up,' Guido stopped her. 'That's the whole point of you wearing it; Max will want to show you off.'

They rolled in under the main gates, which were topped with the family crest, under the heavy wooden portcullis and across the gravelled quad to the entrance where Maggie could see Max waiting. Guido opened the rear door of the car and told her to wait, although it was all she could do to stop herself from running up the stone steps and into her master's arms.

Standing to one side of Max was a very distinguished man who Maggie guessed was their host. Guido took a fine leather lead out of his jacket pocket, snapped it to Maggie's collar and then led her, wearing only the black rubber corset, stockings and high heels up the steps of the house, where he handed the lead to Max.

For the moment Maggie was oblivious to her appearance. She could see the pride on Max's face, and wanted nothing more than to please him, even though it struck her that his was not the look of a lover but of a collector, delighted by the impression his possession would make on others.

Their host smiled. 'Well, damn me, Max, if you haven't done it again, although I suppose after all these years I should expect nothing less.'

'Thank you, Hugh, would you care to inspect her?'

'A little preview?' the man mused appreciatively, eyeing Maggie up and down, and a good slave to her master, she kept her eyes respectfully downcast. 'Yes, of course, that would be most agreeable.'

Max tucked the looped end of the lead between her teeth and she stood as she'd been taught, very still with her hands behind her back, feet apart so that Sir Hugh could examine here.

'What very nice breasts,' he said, cupping first one and then the other in his palms, brushing the nipples with his thumbs, the treacherous little buds hardening instantly under his touch. 'Very nice indeed.' He nodded appreciatively and dropped a hand to her flat tummy, and then lower to the mound of her sex, a single finger parting the wet lips of her quim, working lower to enter her.

'Hmm... nice and tight here,' he considered. 'And what about her delightful bottom?'

'You'll find it's in a similar condition,' Max assured him. 'She might need a little stretching yet if one would want to use her regularly, but she is very willing, very eager to please, and very nicely spirited, too. She's actually good company, unlike some I've trained. What more could a devoted master want?'

Sir Hugh nodded sagely, his eyes narrowing as he

considered and concurred with Max's words. Then he withdrew his finger and touched it to his lips, then sucked it, appearing to savour the taste and fragrance like a connoisseur considering a fine wine or a Cuban cigar.

'But is she presentable?' he asked, his eyes holding hers as he addressed Max.

'That goes without saying, Hugh.' Max took Maggie's lead again. 'Now would you object if I took her upstairs and got her settled?'

'Good God, not at all man!' Sir Hugh bellowed good-naturedly. 'Thank you for letting me have first view of your latest acquisition. I'll see you later – I promised Monty that I'll try out his new pony team.'

As he left Max stroked her cheek. 'Well done,' he said. 'I know Sir Hugh, and I know you made a good impression on him.' The compliment made Maggie feel warm inside and surprisingly secure, considering where they were and why they were there. 'Now, we have a suite in the west wing. I suggest we go upstairs, unpack, have a little something to eat and then explore the house. There are things here that will be very new to you. The whole house, in fact the whole estate, is a hedonist's paradise. The auction always generates a lot of interest and even those who aren't buying or selling like to come along and, well, exhibit, meet old friends, catch up, show off a little. But before we put you on the block there are some things I'd like you to see.'

Maggie looked at him questioningly, knowing her expression betrayed her apprehension.

Max pulled her close to him. 'Don't be afraid, my little one,' he comforted. 'I won't let anything happen to you that you're not ready for.'

Maggie held her tongue; despite wanting to tell him that she wasn't sure if she was ready for anything the rambling house may have in store for her.

Inside the main door the hall opened up into a huge galleried space. Even though it was summer a log fire burned in a large fireplace. The area was lined with panelling and hung with ancestral portraits, and she could see the family resemblance between the faces depicted in the oil paintings and Sir Hugh. It was a magnificent reception area that implied permanence and a sense of unbroken husbandry.

In stark contrast to the gravitas of the surroundings, on stone plinths either side of the fire stood two iron cages, like oversized bird cages, and in each was standing a naked man, hooded, wrists manacled together behind their backs. Their cocks and balls were encased in a series of leather and metal hoops that held them in a state of semi-erection. Beside one cage a tall bald man dressed in a white ball gown and silver high heels was feeding one of the caged slaves grapes on the end of a long stick.

In open-mouthed awe Maggie followed Max towards the sweeping staircase, finding it impossible not to glance to one side through open double doors into what looked like a ballroom. It was full of people, some naked, some dressed, the general hubbub drifting out to meet them. That gave her some idea of how big an event the auction was. The hall seemed to be full of people mingling, talking – masters, mistresses and their slaves, dressed in all manner of costumes or naked except for collars and chains.

Max, following her gaze, smiled. 'All in good time, my dear,' he said. 'All in good time. Let's go upstairs and get settled first.'

Maggie hadn't realised how hungry she was until she got to the room. In a handsome suite that overlooked the deer park someone had laid out a cold buffet on one of the side tables. She must have looked at the delicious spread with hungry eyes, for Max, taking a crop from the desk, said, 'First things first, my dear. First things first…'

He approached her. 'I am delighted to see you're correctly dressed,' he said. 'I want you well marked before you go on the block tomorrow.' He indicated the sofa. 'Now bend over.'

Maggie hesitated; she had a love-hate relationship with the crop, and other implements Max used on her. She hated being beaten and yet at the same time she loved it. It was a shock to know that it turned her on in a way like nothing else did. She realised with a terrible sense of surety that anticipating her punishment, enduring it, and revelling in the memory of it afterwards was one of the most exciting parts of her relationship with Max. It was a symbol quite unlike any other of just how much she was prepared to give to him. Combined with the sexual pleasure and sense of total submission and humiliation this subtle game was quite unlike anything she had ever experienced.

She took a deep breath, turning her thoughts inward, gathering herself in some secret place that allowed her to relish and ride the pain. She heard the crop cut through the still air and gasped as the leather cracked raw and angry across her buttocks. 'One!' she snorted. He hit her harder than she'd anticipated and the first stroke brought tears to her eyes.

'There is no need to count, my dear,' he informed her, and she wondered if that meant he would go on until she could take no more?

The crop found its mark again. This time Maggie shrieked, but before she could recover he hit her again. After six his fingers massaged the glowing flesh, a mixed blessing for although she was delighted by his touch, at the same time rubbing made the blood flow all the faster through the welts.

At twelve he stopped again and Maggie whimpered, rubbing her head against his steadying arm.

'I'm going to miss you so much, Maggie,' he stated, and held the crop out for her to kiss.

Stunned, she murmured her thanks, her heart aching.

Max helped her to her feet. 'Now go and tidy yourself up and eat, we have a long night ahead of us.'

He smiled indulgently while she ate a very late lunch. As she gazed out of the window a small cart trundled by on the gravel path below, and then another. Maggie watched them, and then realised with a start that they were being pulled by women – heavily built naked women, with plumed headdresses, harnesses and bells, trotting in step, whipped on by a liveried driver. They were matched pairs and fours, some blinkered, all turned out as smartly as any show ponies she had ever seen.

Max stood behind her and handed her a glass of champagne. 'Pony girls,' he said, in answer to her unspoken question. 'They are Sir Hugh's particular passion... those two in the front are identical Swedish twins. All trained, bred, beaten, treated as close to the real thing as he can manage. He likes more sophisticated creatures for the house, although in other most households pony girls double as house slaves or bed mates.'

'Will I end up as a pony girl?' she asked uneasily.

Max shook his head. 'Unlikely,' he said. 'Possible, but unlikely. You'll be sold as a companion body slave. A decorative creature to share a discerning man's bed and maybe his life.'

Max adjusted the rubber corset so that her buttocks were shown off to their best advantage, the marks of the crop still red and fierce, and then he rolled down the bra cups so that her breasts were fully exposed.

Maggie stared at him as he picked up the crop again. He smiled thinly and she cringed. 'Put your hands behind your neck,' he ordered, and Maggie felt an icy chill grip her, guessing what was about to follow.

He stroked the loop of the crop under her chin and then said, as if to still the anxiety and fear in her eyes, 'Six quick strikes, they will hurt and then they'll be done. Do you understand?'

Maggie nodded and closed her eyes in readiness. He was right, they were quick, they did hurt and she screamed as the crop cut across her delicate flesh.

'That looks better,' he said as she squirmed into his arms for comfort. 'Now finish your lunch.'

Half an hour later Max clipped on Maggie's lead and led her back downstairs. Nervous and extremely apprehensive, she felt quite overawed by her surroundings.

On low dais and plinths in the ballroom were all manner of things to bemuse and amuse and electrify the senses. On one was an oiled, naked man, manacled to a great cross. Behind him a muscular coloured master dressed in leather shorts and a full facemask applied a whip with force, raising great welts on the slave's golden skin.

On another dais a small muscular man was hog-tied and suspended from an ornate metal frame. On yet another stood a petite Eurasian girl entirely covered in tattoos, her expression icy cold and empty.

'Are these people all for sale?' Maggie whispered in amazement.

Max's eyes narrowed venomously and Maggie knew she had broken one of the fundamental rules and spoken without permission, but even so she was still horribly curious.

'No,' he snapped, 'some are here for their masters and mistresses to show them off. To put them through their paces, to let us all enjoy their special tricks and skills.'

He pointed across the room to where two beautiful blonde girls in plumes stood strapped into the little cart Maggie had spotted earlier. On either side of the magnificent hearth, in wicker baskets, were two redheaded youths, sitting to attention like two well trained and perfectly matched dogs.

In one corner a large man dressed in no more than leather cuffs and a thong was juggling melons, while alongside him a naked female contortionist, collared and at the end of a fine silver chain, had the undivided attention of at least a couple of dozen men. On a stage three male slaves had weights attached to their balls and a man was taking bets on who would last the longest before calling enough.

They walked slowly along rows of human exhibits, until they finally got to an area that Maggie began to realise was for sale lots.

Eventually it seemed they had reached their destination, where stood a row of women chained to blocks, dressed much as she was in some nominal garment that barely covered their bodies. They were of all sizes and ages, the only common denominator that they all wore collars and were chained to the little dais upon which they stood.

Max led Maggie to an empty dais at the end of the row, and she began to tremble as several of the browsing masters, each with a catalogue in hand, turned their attentions to her.

Max snapped her lead into a ring on the surface of the low dais. 'Don't panic,' he told her. 'I won't leave you and I'll be here tonight if you need me.' Maggie suddenly felt sick and faint. Although she wanted more than anything to please him and show him she was a good slave, this was almost more than she could bear. Her loyalty was to him, and she couldn't imagine being with any of the others who approached the dais and looked her over like prime horseflesh. Would one of these men be her eventual keeper?

'Very nice,' said one of them to Max. 'May I?'

Max lifted a hand in a gesture of invitation. 'You know the rules, Rupert,' he said warmly. 'You may touch but no more. If you would like more then you must register your request with the auctioneer.'

Maggie watched the men come and go from lowered eyes. It seemed they were allowed to inspect her, ask her to turn this way and that, look and carry out a perfunctory inspection, but no more. Max answered what questions they asked, although she guessed that as soon as he felt she was settled he would leave her to her own devices to go and look at what else was on offer.

And she was right, for eventually he nodded and made his way back into the crowd.

Alone and unguarded Maggie kept her eyes demurely downcast, trying hard not to attract attention to herself. She heard one of the men explaining to his companion that if a would-be purchaser wished for more access to any of the lots then their name was added to a list under the lot number. Then the auctioneer decided who got what for the night and whether such an encounter was public or private.

Maggie had finally begun to settle a little when a group of men came in through the double door. They made a noisy entrance, at odds with the polite hum and murmur of conversation that filled the hall. The noise made everyone look up, and instantly Maggie realised with horror that amongst the new arrivals was none other than Simon Faraday!

She immediately dropped her gaze again as she saw him scanning the room, wishing she could make herself invisible. This couldn't be happening. There had to be a mistake. Maybe it was someone who closely resembled him.

She peeped again and then quickly down. No, there was no mistake. It was most definitely Simon Faraday. How on earth could he be there? How was it possible? Simon Faraday showing up was the most unbelievable and worst thing that could possibly happen.

To her horror he caught sight of her, his eyes widening momentarily, and then he smiled triumphantly and sauntered over. He didn't speak, not a word, but instead he arrogantly looked her up and down.

Casually he cast his eye down at the list of bids, marked something on the sheet and then moved away without so much as a word or a backward glance. Maggie shuddered, instinctively aware that there was no way this would be the end of it.

A little while later a man dressed in dark green livery came up to the block. He had a chain fastened to his waist on which hung a large key ring, weighed down with dozens of keys, one of which Maggie assumed would open the lock that attached her lead to the plinth.

'You've been selected by one of our patrons to keep him company for the night,' he said as he bent to unlock her, then straightened up, his eyes greedily devouring her vulnerable beauty.

Maggie suspected that he had his fair share of the goods on show when the masters and mistresses weren't looking. She bit her lip anxiously and glanced around the room, searching for Max, trying to guess who'd had enough influence to secure her already. She had assumed the decisions were made at the end of the day.

He jerked the leash and pulled her down to his level. 'Maybe I'll try you out myself,' he hissed, 'when the master has done with you.'

Maggie shuddered as he slid a cold hand over her thigh and cupped her sex. 'Nice tight arse, nice tight cunt, that's what it says in your auction notes,' he leered, licking his lips. 'Wouldn't mind trying you out for myself...'

Before she could react he clipped a pair of handcuffs on her, then against a backdrop of appreciative looks and comments he led her through the crowd. She reddened, trying hard to block out the crude comments and avaricious stares. It seemed that everyone knew where she was destined, if not with whom. As they reached the doorway she looked around again, frantically trying to spot Max amongst the sea of faces. Did he know she was being taken away? Had he given his permission? Her stomach tightened into a tangled knot of disquiet.

The man led her upstairs, keeping ahead of her so that the lead stayed taut between them. On one of the landings he knocked on an ornate door, and waited for permission to enter.

'Come in,' called a muffled voice, and Maggie took a deep breath to try and steady her nerves. Oddly enough, in some ways it reminded her of her first encounter with Max. Maybe it wouldn't be so bad after all...

'Well, well, just look who we have here,' gloated a familiar voice, and Maggie froze in horror, her worst fears – the ones she'd been trying hard to suppress – confirmed. 'Fancy meeting you here.'

Simon Faraday was lounging on a leather sofa, a glass

of wine in his hand. Another man stood by the fireplace leering at her, both of them looking the worse for drink.

Simon beckoned her closer. 'I genuinely had no idea until I saw you up on the dais that you were involved in our little club,' he said. 'I must be slipping. I knew Max had a new slave in his stable, but I had no idea it could be you. Small world, isn't it, eh Maggie?'

Maggie kept her eyes firmly fixed to the floor as the man who'd delivered her to the suite unlocked her wrists and tucked the lead between her lips.

'Nothing to say for yourself?' Simon taunted. 'My, my, my, isn't that something? I think this is the quietest I've ever known you. Now strip, I want to see again what's on offer. One fumbled fuck on the bathroom floor hardly counts as a fair appraisal.'

Maggie was quite unable to move, and then she heard another familiar voice. 'You know better than to behave like this, young lady,' said Max Jordan, and she glanced round in astonishment to see him sitting in the window seat sipping a glass of champagne. She almost cried with relief, even though his expression was stern. 'Don't keep my associate waiting.'

Reluctantly, feeling somewhat betrayed, she unfastened the suspenders from the stockings and peeled down the corset. Simon nodded his approval, indicated she should turn around, and Maggie did so, aware of his eyes crawling over her flesh.

Putting down his wine, rising and stepping closer, he smiled. Maggie waited, and then without warning he reached out and snagged his fingers in her hair, pulling her close, kissing her aggressively. 'I'm going to make you wish you'd been more cooperative with me,' he threatened ominously. 'We all know that Max spends a long time getting the best out of his girls, a mixture of cruelty and kindness pushing the limits. Let's see just how far you've come, shall we? And if you're really lucky, well, who knows what tomorrow might bring? I could do with a new slave.'

He sniggered and dragged her through into the adjoining bedroom, where he threw her on the bed, slightly knocking the wind out of her. His silent companion followed them in and closed the bedroom door, separating her from Max.

She gasped for breath. 'Don't hurt me, Simon,' she pleaded miserably. 'I'll do whatever you want, I promise.'

'Oh, I know you will, it's just a shame you didn't think of that earlier.' He grabbed her breasts, squeezing them tight until she gasped with pain. A part of her believed that any moment now Max would come in and rescue, but realistically she knew he wouldn't. But nevertheless his presence meant that Simon wouldn't go too far, she was sure of that, and retribution would be milder than he might inflict if left to his own devices.

'Get on the bed and lie on your front,' he ordered. 'I'm going to show you just who is the real master around here.'

She did as she was told, trembling as Simon and his unknown friend bound her hand and foot, tying her down spread-eagled on the brocade quilt. Then Maggie heard something cut the air and screamed in shock as a cat-o'-nine tails exploded across her buttocks.

'Shall I gag her?' asked his companion, his tone sinister.

'No, no,' Simon stopped him. 'I like to hear her scream.'

Maggie's body convulsed as he struck again, the spiteful leather fronds wrapping around the soft flesh of her thighs and flanks. There was no mercy and she cried out again and again as the cat found its mark. At last he was done and untied her, pulled her up onto all fours and without ceremony fed his throbbing cock deep into her cunt; an act of glorious conquest.

Maggie was too tired and too shocked to resist him. He pulled her back against his groin, thrusting deeper and deeper, and then he bucked twice and filled her with his seed. Then rolling to the side onto his back pulled her down to him, smiling as he stroked her hair away from her tearstained face.

'I think my friend has need of you now,' he said. 'And then I'm going to roll you over and lick your little cunt until you scream for me to stop. You need to get used to my friend and the things we both like. I intend to bid for you at the auction, so just think, by this time tomorrow you could be all mine.'

As Maggie tried to absorb the enormity of what she'd been fearful of hearing, she felt the other man clamber onto the bed behind her. He slipped his fingers into her wet sex, and then smeared Simon's sperm and her juices up over the tightly puckered closure of her bottom, and she gasped as he probed with his cock and eased it into her tight rear passage.

Beneath her Simon smiled victoriously, and then got up onto his knees, and holding the back of her head he pressed his flaccid cock to her mouth. 'I want you to clean me up now, bitch,' he ordered. 'Just like Max taught you. Suck me, and who knows, by the time my friend here is finished with you I might be ready to fuck you again myself.

Chapter Thirteen

When Simon and his quiet friend were done with

Maggie, Max Jordan clipped her lead on and took her back to his suite. Although she was sore and tired, as soon as the doors were closed behind them she felt the tension easing, but it seemed her ordeal was not quite over.

Max slid his belt from the loops of his trousers. 'I'm very disappointed with you, Maggie,' he said, folding the belt in two.

She was about to protest, but knew it was pointless and would make things worse, not better.

'I thought you understood the first rule a good slave learns is total obedience?'

She nodded, but he grabbed her hair and pulled her head back so that he was looking deep into her eyes. 'It's not good enough, my dear. You know better than to nod. What is the first rule a good slave learns?'

'Obedience, master,' she said, gasping as he jerked her head back further still.

'And trust? Haven't I told you that I will always look after you?'

'But what if Simon buys me at auction tomorrow?' she protested, oblivious now of the punishment she might incur for speaking without permission.

Max snorted and shook his head. 'Relax, Maggie, Simon isn't the only one with friends in high places.'

'But he managed to get me taken to his room tonight.'

Max smiled knowingly. 'Indeed he did, my dear. And how do you think he did that?'

Her eyes widened in terrible comprehension. 'You?' she gasped. 'You arranged for Simon to have me?' If this had been a test then Maggie knew she had failed miserably. 'I'm so sorry,' she whispered meekly.

'You know that slaves aren't allowed to be sorry; it implies they have self-will. So now you have to beg forgiveness, young lady.'

She looked up at him, eyes brimming with tears. 'Please, master,' she whispered, 'forgive me, please.'

Max stroked her face. 'You are very special to me, Maggie, but you know the rules. Get on your hands and knees.'

She did, trembling furiously, but even so she had a sense of relief; with Max she did understand the rules, she knew exactly what was expected and against all the odds she did trust him implicitly – it was the rest of the world she doubted.

Max ran a hand over her bottom as if to settle her. Then Maggie heard the belt cutting through the still air, heard the gasp, felt the red-hot glow of pain as it spread through her body, fused with the sense of well-being, of coming home, of being safe.

The belt found the mark again, this time she shrieked and as she did Max hit her harder and then harder still, on and on until she was lost in the overpowering sensations.

When he was done Maggie heard the belt drop to the floor, heard the sound of his zipper and an instant later the drive of his raging cock sinking into her sex, and then she cried out in a mixture of discomfort and pleasure as he pressed fully into her. She threw back her head and cried out his name, sobbing with pure delight as he drove into her again and again.

While Max fucked her, cruelly forcing his cock deeper and deeper into her cunt, Maggie moved with him, hungrily desperately. For all the world it felt to her as if he was claiming back what, at least until tomorrow, was his.

Hours later Maggie woke in Max's bed, curled up in his arms, his hand cupping her breast, his breath warm and reassuring on the back of her neck. For a moment or two she felt at perfect peace, until her mind cleared and she realised that today was the day of the auction.

What if Max was wrong? What if Simon somehow managed to buy her after all? What if some unknown buyer stepped in? What would her life become without Max Jordan?

She closed her eyes, praying for sleep to reclaim her but her stirring had disturbed Max. For the last time she turned slowly in his arms and wriggled down the bed, he turned sleepily to allow her to move and then gently she drew his flaccid cock into her mouth.

It was bliss, he was soft and warm, the skin of his sleeping cock like silk against her tongue and yet still with the promise of more. Slowly, very slowly he began to harden at the same time as stirring into wakefulness. Max moaned with pleasure as she stoked his balls, paying special attention to the sensitive area between them and his anus. He murmured, opening his legs to give her greater access. Eagerly she licked up over his shaft, and when he was powerfully rigid she eased onto her side, pulled one leg up, and still warm from sleep and barely conscious he guided his cock into her from behind, her body opening to him like a blossoming flower.

He thrust deeper, groaning softly as her body welcomed him. 'That feels good,' he whispered, voice still thick with sleep. 'I'm going to miss you, Maggie,' he mumbled, and inched deeper still. Maggie shivered as he pulled her hips back to him, his desire increasing with consciousness. As he began to find his rhythm she struggled to hold back the tears. After a few moments he rolled onto his back, bringing her with him, still joined, so that she was on her back, lying on him. 'Touch yourself, Maggie,' he whispered, moving her fingers over her clit while still easing in and out of her.

Her body hummed as her fingers echoed in time with the rhythm of his thrusts. She began to gasp for breath, feeling her sex tighten around his thick shaft, driving them both forward into oblivion.

A while later, showered and perfumed and exquisitely made-up, Maggie followed Max down into to the ballroom, dressed in a black silk basque, seamed black silk stockings and high heels. The basque, a final present from Max, emphasised her narrow waist and rounded hips, the suspenders framing her naked sex. She knew it was a look he favoured.

Max walked slowly down the stairs and into the melee in the large room, letting the gathered purchasers take a long hard look at his prize possession. Maggie kept her eyes down at the floor as they made their way amongst them, three paces behind him wearing her collar and leash. He led her backstage where a line of girls was already waiting in silence, their eyes wide with trepidation and nerves.

Max smiled and stroked her cheek. 'If ever you need me,' he said, 'simply give me a ring. You still have the mobile I gave you?'

Maggie nodded, unable to find the words she longed to say.

'Good,' he said. 'Well, in that case I have to leave you now.'

'Leave?' she echoed timorously, and as she spoke the man who'd delivered her to Simon the day before pulled her into line, unfastened her collar and handed it back to Max. 'W-what do you mean, leave?' she stammered as the man slipped another plain leather band around her throat. 'You didn't say anything about leaving.'

'You really must learn to be quiet, Maggie, it's going to get you into so much trouble,' Max said, taking the collar the old man offered him. 'I've business to see to back in town. But don't worry, Guido will be here to keep an eye on you.'

Guido? Maggie felt faint. 'But...' she began, and then stopped. What was there left to say? He kissed her cheek, the kiss as chaste as one given by an ageing uncle to a favourite niece. 'Good luck, my little one,' he said. 'Ring me if you need to.'

At least he didn't say goodbye, but Max Jordan turned and was gone. Maggie felt terribly alone, but immediately the man handcuffed her hands behind her back, and before she could protest he dragged her across the stage and added her to the line of girls waiting to be led to the block. At the head of the queue were two tall blonde women, dressed in black studded leather bra and shorts, and who led each lot out onto the stage to the auction proper. As the curtain rose and fell Maggie caught a glimpse of the buyers standing in the main hall.

As an Asian girl made her way up onto the block, Maggie caught sight of Mike and Kay standing amongst the onlookers, and behind them Simon Faraday, programme in hand.

Slowly, inexorably, the queue of lots shuffled forward, the air heavy with perfume. Maggie's stomach began to churn and she wished for the all the world there was somewhere to hide, somewhere to run to. Simon, she knew, was just as dogged as Max but without his worldly sophistication might play dirtier. And what about Guido? Although Max had said he was merely there to keep an eye on her, hadn't he said he might try and buy her too? The first slave in a new master's stable. Guido hadn't any of Max's surety and was cruel by contrast.

After what seemed like an eternity the two leather-clad women took charge of Maggie. She could feel her heart beating in her chest and felt sick and faint as the curtains parted. She could see Mike looking her up and down and studying the catalogue, and momentarily she caught Simon's eye. He grinned with all the warmth of a basking shark.

'Lot twenty-five,' announced the auctioneer. 'Slave Maggie trained by Max Jordan. Good breasts.' One of the women cupped her soft tits in her hands and tweaked the nipple erect while her twin sucked the other, Maggie blushing furiously. 'Good and tight...' he reported, and one of the women slipped a leather-clad finger deep into her sex, Maggie gasping as the woman's thumb brushed her clitoris. 'Very responsive,' the auctioneer continued. 'Who wouldn't be delighted to find a nice little bitch like this tied to the end of their bed every morning?' There was ripple of laugher as the man picked up his gavel 'Turn around,' he said to Maggie, indicating the required movement with his hand.

Blushing furiously she turned slowly under the watchful gaze of countless pairs of eyes, and when her back was to them the auctioneer said, 'Bend over and hold the frame.' She did as she was told, at which point one of the leather-clad women spread her legs and pulled apart her buttocks to reveal both her sex and the tight puckering of her anus. The woman then slipped a finger back into her sex to murmurs of approval from the audience.

'And so, what am I bid for lot twenty-five?' asked the auctioneer, tapping his gavel on the desk. 'Who will start the bidding? You sir?'

Maggie, glancing back over her shoulder, saw Simon raise a hand and heard him make an opening bid. Slowly she closed her eyes, praying for a miracle.

Max picked up his mobile to take the call.

'She's just gone up onto the block,' Guido reported.

'Good,' said Max, and glanced out of the window at the rolling countryside. 'It shouldn't be long now then. I take it there's much interest in her.'

'Like bees round a honeypot,' the disembodied voice confirmed. 'I'll ring you when the sale is over, shall I, sir?'

'Yes, fine,' Max said thoughtfully, and then before he could hang up he added, 'just wait a minute, Guido.'

Up on the block Maggie tried hard to blank out the stream of rising numbers, tried hard to blank out the sounds of the voices calling their bids. It was all too much. She felt dizzy and sick, the room was hot and noisy, the bidders, although not boisterous or crude, where hungry and excited. From the corner of her eye she could see Guido watching her with avid interest.

Meanwhile the last man left bidding against Simon pulled out. 'So, going once... going twice...' called the auctioneer, lifting the gavel. Maggie froze... and then above the murmur of the onlookers she heard Guido add another two hundred pounds to the previous bid.

Maggie relaxed a little, but still had mixed feelings; a relief that at least Simon Faraday had some competition, but anxiety too. Did she want to be owned by Max's driver? Would he be any better than Faraday? Surely he wouldn't really buy her? She had no idea what he did when not in Max's service, but could he afford her? What would her life be like with Guido?

Simon upped the price again, a glint in his eyes and determination giving his voice a real edge.

Guido added another two hundred, at which point Simon looked round in total disgust. A hush fell in the room as the onlookers began to realise that there was a real battle of wills going on.

'The bid is against you, sir,' the auctioneer said to Simon.

'I know that,' Simon snapped angrily, and added another two hundred.

The auctioneer raised his eyebrows at Guido, inviting another bid, and Guido nodded and added two hundred more, and this time Simon threw up his hands in disappointment.

'No slave is worth that,' he growled, and turning his back on the stage stalked furiously out of the auction room.

Maggie didn't know whether to laugh of cry. Had Guido really bought her? The price was ridiculous. One of the ushers helped her down from the stage and then led her away to a backroom to await collection. A few minutes later Guido walked in, then passed a docket to the man keeping watch over the newly bought lots.

'You had better be worth the money, that's all I can say,' grumbled Guido, snapping the lead taut and taking her back out into the entrance hall.

'Where are we going?' asked Maggie, anxiously hurrying along behind him as he led her through the old house. Her mind was racing.

Guido looked back over his shoulder and snapped the leash tight 'Quiet!' he ordered. 'You know the rules.'

Maggie shuddered; hadn't Max told her that her mouth would get her into trouble? But there was still something she needed to know, however much it cost her.

'Are you my new master?' she dared to ask.

Guido swung round and pulled her too him, kissing her hard as he cupped her sex. Maggie closed her eyes, submitting totally to his touch. After all, what was the point in resisting, wasn't this exactly what Max had

205

prepared her for, and surely better to be owned by Guido than Simon?

Guido pulled back and smiled at her, almost as if he could sense her finally conceding the fight and giving in. Maggie realised just how much she was going to miss Max. Had Guido finished his training now, too? And if he hadn't and continued to work for Max... she tried to imagine being owned by the servant of the man who trained her. Although at the very least she would perhaps see Max, it would be sweet torture to be with Guido and to watch her true master training another slave.

'Where to now?' she asked, unable to keep the sense of resignation out of her voice.

'Home, slave.'

'Home?' Maggie asked in surprise. 'What do you mean, home?'

'Your new master is waiting for you.'

Maggie frowned. 'But I don't understand,' she said, puzzled. 'What do you mean, my new master? I thought you'd bought me.'

Guido snorted. 'For that price?' he scoffed. 'Don't flatter yourself, Maggie. I'd want half a dozen slaves for what he's just paid.'

'Who then?' she pressed desperately. 'I don't understand.'

Guido pulled open the front door, and there outside on the gravel drive was a familiar car. Maggie felt her heart tighten in her chest, for Max Jordan was at the wheel, the passenger door open, and in his hand he held her collar. Maggie's eyes filled with tears of relief and joy. It seemed she had found her true master after all.

Maggie lay back on the couch staring up at the ceiling. She was naked, with her arms up behind her head, her legs spread wide.

Max smiled down at her. 'I want you marked as mine forever, Maggie,' he said. 'You understand that, don't you?'

She nodded; there was nothing she wanted more, however afraid she was. She bit her lip, only too aware of the balding man working quietly beside the couch preparing his equipment. He looked at Max, who nodded, and with that the man clamped one nipple tight and pulled.

The sensation of the needle passing through the base of the teat took Maggie's breath way and made her cry out in shock and pain, and seconds later he pressed the ring home which made her gasp and then swallow down another cry.

The ring felt cold and alien in her flesh.

'All right?' asked the man, and Maggie nodded bravely, although she wasn't sure whether he was talking to her or to Max. She looked up at her master and saw the delight in his eyes at the sight of the first nipple ring in place. The rings he'd chosen for her were the twins of those worn by his housekeeper, Mrs Griffin, ornate silver hoops around which was a stylised version of his initials. His first slave and his last both marked in the same way, that was what Max had told her the night before as he handed her the tiny jewellery box as a present to mark their first anniversary. Maggie smiled, unsure that she would be his last slave, it seemed unlikely, his hunger for female flesh was legendary. But even so she was deeply touched, and more than that, the rings marked her as his.

Above her the man clamped and then pulled the second nipple taut, Maggie closed her eyes and this time, knowing what to expect, let the pain pass through her along with the needle and the jewellery. But what was to follow next was the piercing she was really afraid of.

Max took hold of her hand. 'I love you, you know that don't you, little one?' he said. Maggie nodded; through all he had done to her and the men and women he had given her to, she still knew it was true. Max loved in a unique and terrifying way.

Between her legs the man clamped the lips of her quim apart and taped them back so that she was totally exposed. With a gloved hand he sterilised the area, clamped and then pulled the hood of her clit. Maggie swallowed hard, trying not to panic, trying not to cry out, and then there was searing pain as the needle passed through the delicate flesh. Maggie grimaced and writhed, desperately clutching Max's hand.

'All done,' said the man, placing the equipment back on the bench.

Maggie opened her eyes and took the mirror the man offered her. She looked amazing; the rings in her nipples looked wonderful, the one in her clitoral hood sensational. Max smiled, and as if he could read her mind, told her, 'It looks magnificent, slave.'